Philipp Röttgers

Two eras of Genesis?

The development of a rock band

Tectum Verlag

Philipp Röttgers

Two eras of Genesis?
The development of a rock band

© Tectum Verlag Marburg, 2015
ISBN: 978-3-8288-3592-4

Umschlagabbildungen:
Band-Foto (Tony Banks, Phil Collins and Mike Rutherford): David
Scheinmann, Wikimedia Commons: https://commons.wikimedia.org/
wiki/File:Genesis_%28UK%29.jpg. Logo: SunOfErat, Wikimedia
Commons: https://commons.wikimedia.org/wiki/File:Genesis_%28
Logo%29.png

Printed in Germany
Alle Rechte vorbehalten

Besuchen Sie uns im Internet
www.tectum-verlag.de

Bibliografische Informationen der Deutschen Nationalbibliothek
Die Deutsche Nationalbibliothek verzeichnet diese Publikation in der
Deutschen Nationalbibliografie; detaillierte bibliografische Angaben sind
im Internet über http://dnb.ddb.de abrufbar.

Philipp Röttgers

Two eras of Genesis?

Table of contents

1. A Call To Arms: Introduction

Take the hits 'Biko' by Peter Gabriel, 'In the Air Tonight' by Phil Collins, 'The Living Years' by Mike and the Mechanics and 'Turn It on Again' by Genesis – what do they have in common apart from being chart hits? Right – they all come out of a group, which, like no other group, had no problem in leading successful band career and successful solo careers parallel for a long time. A group, whose members could have filled the Top 10 Single Charts in a week sometime in the 1980s without any problems!

On June 30, 1990, a concert, introduced as the "biggest British charity event since Live Aid" (Thompson 2005: 239) was played at Knebworth Park in England. It featured many of the greatest musicians of that period, "including Paul McCartney, Eric Clapton, Mark Knopfler, Elton John and Pink Floyd" (Bowler & Dray 1992: 214). But the man of the hour (and of the whole decade that lay behind him) "was Phil Collins, who caught the most admiring eye, as he ran first through a set with his Serious Band and then [...] he augmented that lineup with "my two best friends"", whereupon Tony Banks and Mike Rutherford entered the stage "for a closing 20 minutes of Genesis" (Thompson 2005: 240).

At that point in their history, the members of the band Genesis were "more concerned with solo material than band compositions" (Thompson 2005: 239). Phil Collins was at the peak of his solo career, being more famous for that than for being in Genesis, and releasing hit single after hit single, like 'In The Air Tonight', his "first-ever solo single" with its very own "style, passion, identity – and a pounding rhythm" (Waller 1985: 79) or his cover of "the Motown classic 'You Can't Hurry Love'" (Welch 2005: 109). Guitarist Mike Rutherford was in the charts with his band Mike and the Mechanics, most famous for "'All I Need Is a Miracle', one of the great pop songs of the age" (Welch 2005: 122). Only keyboardist Tony Banks, who collaborated with the likes of "Fish from Marillion", with whom he had released the song 'Shortcut to Somewhere', failed to gain any chart success. Fish's voice was said to resemble the voice of a certain Peter Gabriel (cf. Holm-Hudson 2008: 143), a man who, like Phil Collins, "began to dominate the music industry" by "unleashing a veritable cascade of hit solo albums and singles" (Welch 2005: 4), the most famous probably being "the instantly appealing 'Sledgehammer'" (Welch 2005: 102). Some people in 1990 might have not known that Gabriel had once been in the same band with Collins. Of course, many people knew that they were once together in "what had previously been described as an 'art rock' band" (Welch 2005: 4), especially since Collins & Co. had kept on playing songs like 'I Know What

I Like' or 'The Lamb Lies Down On Broadway' since Gabriel's departure in 1975 (cf. Welch 2005: 92). But more famous were hits and more recent complex tracks like 'Follow You Follow Me', 'Turn It On Again', 'Mama', 'Home By The Sea', 'Invisible Touch', 'Land Of Confusion', 'Tonight Tonight Tonight', 'Throwing It All Away', 'No Son Of Mine', 'Jesus He Knows Me' and 'I Can't Dance', songs that could easily fill a whole *Hits*-compilation. Since Phil Collins had taken over the lead vocals and the band and its members released hit single after hit single, they seemed to have developed from a once great progressive rock band to a simple pop group.

Christopher Curries review of the album *We Can't Dance* from 1991 gives a good overview of the prevailing prejudices that surround the music group Genesis. It was his second review after *The Lamb Lies down on Broadway* from 1975 and in his opinion "both the best and worst Genesis studio albums [were] covered." He calls the album "something of a monstrosity [...], spawning several tedious and idiotic singles that made it almost impossible for fans of progressive music to retain any reasonable level of tolerance for the outfit." And of course, "Phil [Collins] is most deserving of the blame." He finishes his review with the statement that "there really isn't any need for a progressive fan to buy this album."

That is the general view on Genesis, a progressive rock band that had to face the loss of its great singer Peter Gabriel and afterwards changed into a pop band, when drummer Phil Collins took over the microphone. Peter Gabriel was even announced "Prog God" at the progressive rock music awards in 2014 (cf. Masters, n.d.), the band itself had been given a lifetime-award two years earlier, which was accepted by Tony Banks and Mike Rutherford. Genesis' producer Nick Davis (in Banks et al 2007: 331) agrees that "the albums definitely fall into eras." Indeed, the Genesis back catalogue gives a wild range of different songs and styles and seems to part the fan-base into two different camps: The progressive-fan cannot bear listening to Phil Collins' 'One More Night' and the average pop-fan skips over Genesis' epic double album *The Lamb Lies down on Broadway*. He prefers to listen to Phil Collins' 'Another Day in Paradise', while the progressive rock fan would like to hear Peter Gabriel's album *Up*. When he looks into his vinyl collection he might find Genesis' *Wind and Wuthering* but not *Genesis*! But both fans probably have Peter Gabriel's album *Us* in their collection – and both of them can sing along to 'I Know What I Like (In Your Wardrobe)', Genesis' 1973 4-minute single from one of their most progressive albums, *Selling England By The Pound*!

In an article on cracked.com it is said that "the bulk of Genesis' new albums was pop and lots of Phil Collins." Adam Tod Brown admits that "the prevailing historical opinion is that, after taking over frontman duties, Collins proceeded to completely ruin the Genesis legacy, turning the band into wussy music for boring adults, but it's not like Gabriel left and the band released "Invisible Touch" the next day."

A new frontman for an established band is always something that makes the fans insecure. People identify with the singer. When Ozzy Osbourne left Black Sabbath and was replaced by Ronnie James Dio, fans were divided into two camps: The band sounded better, Dio had a better singing voice and wrote mystic lyrics, but one could not bear to hear him sing "Paranoid". Should they have changed their name at that point? Definitely not. Tony Iommi, guitarist of the band from its beginning until today *is* Black Sabbath.

Neo-progressive band Marillion (who were dealt as successors of old Genesis) lost their singer Fish after roughly ten years. They recruited Steve Hogarth and together the band have made music for over 25 years, but the record sells have never reached their early heights again. Should the band have renamed themselves although the musicians were all the same?

And what about the likes of Iron Maiden or Deep Purple, who became famous and successful after their first singers had left? They became famous with singer no. 2 and everyone that followed up could not relive the spirit of the most famous line-up.

An interesting case is Pink Floyd. Their earliest incarnation had Syd Barrett as frontman and songwriter, which made him "Mr. Pink Floyd". He left after two albums only and the band's bassist, Roger Waters, slowly moved himself to the front over the years, claiming to be "Mr. Pink Floyd", even after he had left the band. Next, guitarist David Gilmour took over the role of the front man, seen by many as "Mr. Pink Floyd". How often would this band have had to change their name?

Genesis faced the same problem after the loss of their second vocalist. When Phil Collins, who had "always been Genesis, at least to the record buying public who can't really tell his solo career apart from Genesis" (McMahan 1998: 4) left in 1996, they hired a new vocalist, Ray Wilson, but after his predecessors Gabriel and Collins, he unfortunately had no chance to become "Mr. Genesis". But "Mr. Genesis" was someone else. There are actually two "Mr. Genesis": Keyboardist Tony Banks and guitarist/bassist Mike Rutherford, who founded the band in 1967 and have seen it through all its successes and changes. Barley anyone realized that these two were the driving forces behind a progressive band that was progressive in the truest sense of the word. The focus is and has always been on the two singers and the fans might only think of Banks and Rutherford when wondering: "How did they allow the band to become so poppy?"

We will have a look at "how they could have allowed it". First of all, we will take a look at the musical evolution that surrounded their genesis and then we will go through their history and pick out songs to make up the trademarks that each "era" bears (the Peter Gabriel era runs from 1967-1975, the Phil Collins era runs from 1975-1996). We will see how they changed, *if* they changed, what caused any changes and we will look at how true the accusations against the band are. Another important factor is also the inclusion of the solo careers of the members, which might shed new light on who was responsible for which feature in the band's music and performance. Is it really true, that after Phil Collins became popular with short simple love songs, he took over this recipe on Genesis or are there any other factors one might have to consider?

For the solo careers, I chose songs by each member to point out certain features of their careers. The songs and performances can be found on Youtube, lyrics and album covers are linked. In the beginning of each chapter that deals with a special song or album I added comments from the videos I deal with in that chapter that show the general atmosphere when it comes to discussions about Genesis.

2. The Journey: Musical development in Britain in the early 1960s

> ...different generations, diverse backgrounds, be it musically, politically, sociologically. (Ameri & Schmidt 2013: 7)

It was after the Second World War that young people "became significant for the marketing industry, and clothing, cosmetics, magazines, movies and entertainment were designed for and marketed to them." They had "their own radios and record players, and they listened to and bought recordings of music that reflected their own tastes", music that "became known as *pop music.*" This music, especially "rock and roll, united most teenagers in the late 1950s and early 1960s and it created "a "generation gap" between them and older generations." Pop music "split into niche markets, people of all ages found that the music they listened to marked their identity as strongly as the clothes they wore and the ways they behaved" (Burkholder et al 2005: 896).

Britain's musical export were The Beatles, founded in 1960, who conquered the world with their "British Invasion" and they were followed by "bands such as the Rolling Stones, the Kinks, the Animals, the Who, and Cream." All these bands

> "sought an individual sound, they developed many new styles within the broad tradition of rock: the California style of the Beach Boys; Steppenwolf's *heavy metal* style; the *hard rock* of Led Zeppelin and Aerosmith; the *acid rock* or *psychedelic rock* of Jefferson Airplane; and the *avant-garde rock* of Frank Zappa" (Burkholder et al 2005: 900).

Out of these new styles different genres emerged and each genre "had its own stars, fans, and radio programs, and the popularity of songs in each category was tracked on *charts,* weekly rankings by sales of 45-rpm singles" (Burkholder et al 2005: 896). One of the new genres was the genre of progressive rock. It "emerged in Britain" (Hegarty & Halliwell 2011: 10) by the end of the 1960s. The roots go, as for many genres, back to the Beatles, because "the birth of progressive rock is frequently traced back to the release of [their] 1967 album, *Sgt. Pepper's Lonely Hearts Club Band"* (Hegarty & Halliwell 2011: 31). If one thinks of progressive rock, one "will conjure images of long solos, overlong albums, fantasy lyrics, grandiose stage sets and costumes" (Hegarty & Halliwell 2011: 2). The most famous representatives of progressive rock in the 1970s were "Yes, Genesis, Jethro Tull and Emerson, Lake and Palmer (ELP), [...] King Crimson, Soft

Machine and Van der Graaf Generator." Nowadays a new range of progressive rock bands have become famous, such as "Radiohead, Tool, Muse, The Mars Volta and Porcupine Tree" (Hegarty & Halliwell 2011: 3).

Progressive rock has always been a "highly experimental music [...] in which the musical cultural exchange across regions and national borders was an implicit feature" (Hegarty & Halliwell 2011: 10). The most featured instruments are "the classic electric instruments of rock", as "the electric guitar, electric bass, and electric piano and organ [and] drums" (Holmes 1985: 158). However, a lot of newly established instruments and technical features have been used in progressive rock. The most important instruments for progressive rock were any kind of synthesizer, as the Moog, which was invented Robert Moog in 1964 (cf. Holmes 1985: 29) or the Hammond organ (cf. Holmes 1985: 51), which "appeared on some of the early Beatle songs", but "the group that probably did the most to popularize the Hammond sound was Procol Harum" (Holmes 1985: 160), who were to become one of the first progressive rock bands in the world. They were followed by "other popular organs" like "the Vox Continental (featured by Alan Price of the Animals on "House of the Rising Sun")", the "Farfisa" (Holmes 1985: 159) or "the mellotron", whose first famous player was "Mike Pinder of the Moody Blues" (Holmes 1985: 160), another of the first progressive rock's bands. Other synthesizers include the "Arp 2600, a lightweight, portable synthesizer that captured the fancy of musicians with such divergent interests as Henry Mancini, Pete Townshend of the Who, and John Lennon", the "Oberheim (which introduced one of the first polyphonic synthesizers in 1975), Roland, Korg, and EMS" (Holmes 1985: 84). Although "most historians believe that the importance of the piano peaked in the nineteenth century and that the twentieth century has seen a gradual decline in popularity and significance" (Gordon 1996: 530), a number of electric pianos such as "the Fender Rhodes, the Clavinet [...] and models made by Wurlitzer, Yamaha, Crumar, and Hohner [...] were commonly used by both rock and jazz keyboardists" (Holmes 1985: 159). String instruments like guitars and basses were technically innovated by "Adolph Rickenbacker", which "led to the proliferation of guitars and effects that can be achieved with modern instruments of this type." The most famous model of the rock guitar is "the Fender Stratocaster" (Holmes 1985: 159). In general, the "guitar playing in the 1950s and the early 1960s exploited the newly commercially available electric guitar through solos and overdriving of amplifiers" (Hegarty & Halliwell 2011: 25).

Typical features of progressive rock are "talented, skilful and creative" (Hegarty & Halliwell 2011: 9) musicians, whose "virtuosity spread into

12

group composition, sometimes at the cost of musical individualism", concept albums, which allow "scope for narrative, for genre mixing, for instrumental development […] and for lyrical complexity that [is] not possible in shorter form or even in single extended tracks" (Hegarty & Halliwell 2011: 65) as well as "theatricality in the performances" (Hegarty & Halliwell 2011: 51). Jerry Luck (in Halbscheffel 2013: 25) tries to give a list of elements of progressive rock, some of which are:

- "complex arrangements usually featuring intricate keyboard and guitar playing
- Songs predominantly on the longish side, but structured, rarely improvised
- A mixture of loud passages, soft passages, and musical crescendos to add to the dynamics of the arrangements
- The use of Mellotron or string synth to simulate an orchestra backing
- Extended instrumental solos, electric and electronic instruments where each plays a vital role in translating the emotion of compositions which typically contain more than one mood.
- Multi-movement compositions that may or may not return to a musical theme. In some cases the end section may bear little resemblance to the first part of the song.
- Compositions created from unrelated parts, i.e. Genesis' 'Supper's Ready'"

John J. Sheinbaum (in Halbscheffel 2013: 26) adds some more points:

- "focus on keyboards; acoustic versus electric sections
- Rhythm & meter: Syncopations, tricky rhythms; less reliance on 4/4 time signature
- Harmonic progression: Less reliance on 'three-chord' songs, and the simplest chords
- Lyrical material: Mythology, nature, utopia versus technology, modernism; surrealism
- Visual material: Elaborate surrealistic album covers; elaborate stage shows
- Form: Embellishment of traditional shapes (AABA, verse-chorus), less reliance on traditional shapes; unconventional forms
- Site: Towards the mind; less focus on the (dancing) body
- Historical period: Considered 'flourishing' in the early- to mid-1970s

- Historical setting: Originally southern England, especially the London area
- Gender: Primarily male musicians; primarily male audience."

Progressive rock's success and popularity was over, when punk rock arrived. It

> was born in 1976 from a fury of destruction and renewal, and its principal target was progressive rock, whose alleged self-indulgence and pretension would be brought to a close by the fresh and angry authenticity of a newly stripped-down version of rock, invigorated through simplicity. (Hegarty & Halliwell 2011: 1)

Still, the impact of the evolution of rock music since the mid-1960s had left its mark on music history. During that time, "there arose a number of influential groups and individuals, who would prove to have a lasting effect on the aesthetics of rock", namely famous artists like "the Beatles, Jimi Hendrix, Frank Zappa, Pink Floyd, and countless others" (Holmes 1985: 168). Another band that deserves to be named in this row is Genesis, a band, "which in the late 1960s was a fledging progressive band from Charterhouse School in Surrey" (Hegarty & Halliwell 2011: 58), where four boys named Peter Gabriel, Anthony Banks, Michael Rutherford and Anthony Phillips were trying to break away from the unendurable private school routine.

3. The development of the rock band Genesis
Part I: The Peter Gabriel era

3.1 In The Beginning: 1967-1971

god gabriel was beautiful, I will always love Genesis more with him
(youtube-user thatSLAYER chick's comment on the video "Genesis Piper
Club Rome 18 April 1972)

Mike Rutherford: "We like audiences that sit down and listen to the music
rather than get drunk and pic up girls ... We like audiences that sit down
and listen to us." This is the greatest comment on Rock.
(youtube-user Harold.not.the.Barrel's comment on the same video)

The 'classic' Genesis line-up for most fans is the line-up Peter Gabriel
(vocals), Tony Banks (keyboards), Mike Rutherford (bass and guitars),
Steve Hackett (guitar) and Phil Collins (drums). However, before this line-
up came together, Genesis released two albums. Besides the rotating
drummer's seat (three drummers played in the group before Phil Collins
took place), the role of the guitarist was filled out by Anthony Phillips, who
founded Genesis together with Gabriel, Banks and Rutherford when they
were at Charterhouse School, "a leading public school founded in 1611 on
the site of a former 'charterhouse' (Carthusian monastery) in London, but
in 1872 transferred to Surrey" (Room 1990: 64). Unfortunately, his stay with
the band did not last long enough to breathe the air of success, but Peter
Gabriel still calls him "one of the most musical, if not *the* most musical
member of Genesis" (Gabriel 2007: 163). Indeed, Phillips shaped the sound
of early Genesis very much. He himself mentions "all the twelve-string
guitar work that Mike and I had created together" (Phillips 2007: 84).

Banks, Gabriel and Rutherford were all born in 1950, Phillips in 1951
(cf. Fielder 1984: 8). When they were at Charterhouse, Phillips and
Rutherford were playing in a band "called the Anon", Banks and Gabriel
had formed "the Garden Wall". That was very rebellious and Rutherford
had even "been banned from playing the guitar" (Fielder 1984: 16) for some
time. It was the time when "The Beatles came along" (Phillips 2007: 16),
who released hit singles like 'I Wanna Hold Your Hand' almost weekly and
'Swinging London', which included "the whole exciting world of hippies
and Carnaby Street and *Rave* magazine" (Fielder 1984: 15), as Gabriel
remembers. The Beatles were a big influence on all four of them, Tony
Banks and especially Peter Gabriel were fans of Otis Redding (cf. Bright
1988: 24), but they also liked classic music (cf. Fielder 1984: 14 f.). There was

a "piano in the dining hall", which "Banks generally claimed [...] so Peter would sing along with him, although at that time he had no pretensions towards singing, being far more interested in playing the drums" (Bowler & Dray 1992: 9). It happened that "Phillips and Rutherford asked Tony Banks to play Farfisa organ" on a demo of their songs, where Phillips was "to sing lead vocals" (Platts 2007: 10). Phillips remembers that "Banks brought along Peter Gabriel to do one song of theirs (*She is Beautiful*)" and "it was decided that Gabriel would sing lead on all the material" (Platts 2007: 11).

So they recorded their first demo 'She Is Beautiful' and were given the opportunity to record an album (cf. Phillips 2007: 28). When the band started to write music in 1967, Phillips points out that "it wasn't yet the progressive era", but they were already "writing long, rambling pieces" (Platts 2007: 12), something that should become one of the band's trademarks. The music "revealed a band working within mid'-60s pop conventions, with a touch of psych, yet grasping for something more" (Platts 2007: 12). Thompson (2005: 14) thinks that

> "the most significant of these early recordings was "The Mystery of Flannan Isle Lighthouse", one of the earliest ever manifestations of the mighty epics that would soon become one of Genesis's best-loved calling cards – albeit in little more than two-and-a-half minutes."

Their first record *From Genesis to Revelation*, which also gave the group its name, was created and produced by Jonathan King, their "impresario", a young producer who went to the same school as the group. King liked "in particular Gabriel's voice" (Platts 2007: 11), but "wasn't overly impressed by their first demos, until Banks and Gabriel came up with [...] a Bee Gees-style effort called 'The Silent Sun'", which became "their début single" (Welch 2005: 9). The album itself was based on the subject of "the creation of the world, as told in *The Bible* and the subsequent evolution of Mankind" as music journalist Chris Welch (2005: 8) remembers and he adds that "it was bit like a local film club attempting to re-make *Ben Hur* for their first movie project." Jonathan King preferred "the three-minute pop single", but Anthony Phillips said, that "we weren't so much into the more poppy area" (Platts 2007: 13). This can be heard on a song like 'The Serpent' with its "dramatic use of silence" that is "showing that Genesis knew all about the value of dynamics quite early on their evolution", as Chris Welch (2005: 11) puts it. He even thinks that they were taking their "first tentative steps in a musical direction they were determined to pursue" and sees parallels to their later concept album *The Lamb Lies Down On Broadway*. Ironically Peter Gabriel sings: "Beware the future!"

They were still searching for their style and "the so-called progressive rock boom [...] was still in the future" (Thompson 2005: 16). But it was coming fast since they were working on a so-called 'Concept album', which is "synonymous with progressive rock" (Hegarty & Halliwell 2011: 65). The "album could not command any attention" (Welch 2005: 12), the "single releases [...] also failed to chart" (Welch 2005: 11) and this "ended the relationship with Jonathan King" (Welch 2005: 10) and the band signed at Tony Stratton-Smith's label "Charisma" (cf. Thompson 05: 35) to produce their next album. Charisma would later become famous as one of the major labels for progressive rock in Britain (cf. Hegarty & Halliwell 2011: 10 f.). Gail Colson, assistant of Tony Stratton-Smith, remembers of Genesis "as posh little public schoolboys" (in Dodd 2007: 89), an image that would change very soon afterwards. They were not dependent from the producer's taste in music anymore and since they had been on the road for a while (the album came out in 1970) "every song on the album had been performed on stage." The band had spent the winter of 1969/70 in the so-called 'Christmas Cottage', a house owned by road manager Richard MacPhail's parents, to write the songs (cf. Rutherford 2007: 49). They were "trying to do something different, that nobody else was doing at the time, which was extended pieces" (Welch 2005: 17 f.). Their 12-string-guitar sound created a "folk-rock fusion", which "was very important for bands that wanted to move away from the short, tightly constrained song structure of the pop single" (Hegarty & Halliwell 2011: 58). The album was to be called *Trespass* and showed their first "distinctive and attractive cover work art", which should be continued on the following albums. These "elaborate surrealistic album covers" (Sheinbaum in Halbscheffel 2013: 26) were to become typical of progressive rock covers.

Musically, the group had evolved. They included orchestral arrangements, tempo changes and dramatic climaxes in the song 'Looking for someone', and an ebb and flow of moods and themes in the song 'Visions of Angels' (cf. Welch 2005: 18 f.). Lyrically, Peter Gabriel sang about "foxes and wolves and kings" in 'White Mountain', making it a "picturesque story", something that should be continued on the following records. His voice added "a feeling of angst and desperation" (Welch 2005: 19) in 'Visions of Angels'. Hegarty & Halliwell (2011: 58) think that "minstrelsy is evoked by the timbre of Peter Gabriel's vocals, through Gabriel's flute (used less sparingly and more melodically then Ian Anderson's flute) and in the mythological figures that populate the band's early songs." Anthony Phillips and Mike Rutherford played their acoustic guitars "with apparent ease" (Welch 2005: 20) in the song 'Dusk'. Genesis had found their early sound and style on this record. The most notable songs however were 'Stagnation' and 'The Knife'. Pieces of 'Stagnation' can be heard from 0:14 onwards here: https://www.youtube.com/watch? v=XcnkjvHXwaU, in a live video from 1972 from Rome. Phil Collins and Steve Hackett have already taken their places on drums and guitar at this stage. The song 'Stagnation' "is presented in all its glory to very attentive ears, and as usual is one of the highlight of the show" (Russell 2004: 24), including "one of the tactics of Genesis' quickly developing stage act at this time to play gentle acoustic guitar numbers with tinkling piano in the background to lull onlookers into believing they were hearing a folk group [00:14 – 03:56]" (Welch 2005: 19). Afterwards "the band would gradually add lead guitar and drums until they reached a roaring, aggressive climax [03:56 – 04:41]". Welch especially points out the line "I want a drink to wash out the filth" (04:20) that Peter "sings [...] mysteriously before this minor epic sweeps towards a grand finale." Gabriel himself sees the song as "archetypical early Genesis" (Fielder 1984: 30). The footage from Rome is in a way interesting, as Italy was the first country where the band became famous (cf. Fielder 1984: 60). The band kept their special relationship with the country for years. When they finished their last European tour in 2007 in Rome, they played a free concert at Circus Maximus.

'The Knife' "was the most powerful and exciting arrangement Genesis had developed thus far and it became hugely popular at live shows", being a heavy rock number that went through a lot of changes with quiet and heavy bits with distorted guitar and Hammond organ and Peter Gabriel's flute. Welch (2005: 82) calls it the "most violent and psychotic of Genesis works." This was the direction in which Genesis would develop. Besides creating the 12-string guitar sound, Anthony Phillips "was involved in parts of writing of *The Knife* and some of the heavier stuff" (Platts 2007: 30). Gabriel wrote out of his own perspective as "a public schoolboy rebelling against my background" (Fielder 1984: 29). During the making of the album the band had to decide between 'The Knife' or 'Going Out To Get You', another stage favourite (cf. Platts 2007: 29).

Genesis's early sound (even on the following record) is described by Armando Gallo, their photographer and biographer in the 1970s, who says: "...to me they were very old, they were coming from a very old age and at the same time they were so young!" (cf. *Genesis: Songbook Part 1*, 07:39 – 07:48) Indeed, the band has something very British, very old and pastoral, even "Victorian" in their early music, which might be led to their family backgrounds and their educational backgrounds at the private school. This style would change in the future, when Ant Phillips was gone and new members from other backgrounds would join the band. John Silver, the band's drummer on *From Genesis to Revelation,* remembers the way the band worked:

> "Ant Phillips was a very important voice in the style and manner of what we were doing [...] He and Mike I think of as a unit coming up with ideas, ways of doing things. [...] Tony was the guy who would be forming the whole structure because he was the pianist and he had the Farfisa organ; [...] Tony always was the musical heavyweight of the band, no question about it and the most musically prominent. Peter was the singing and the voice" (in Dodd: 2007: 69)

If one takes the lists from Jerry Luck and John J. Sheinbaum that try to pin down the features of progressive rock and changes them a bit, one can make a list of the features of Genesis music in this early stage of the band:

- A mixture of loud passages, soft passages, and musical crescendos to add to the dynamics of the arrangements (as in 'The Knife' and 'Visions of angels')
- Extended instrumental solos, electric and electronic instruments where each plays a vital role in translating the emotion of compositions which typically contain more than one mood (as in 'The Knife')
- Acoustic versus electric sections ("twelve-string guitar" vs. the Hammond organ)
- Less reliance on 'three-chord' songs, and the simplest chords ("the avoidance of pop songs")
- Very "picturesque" and storytelling lyrics: Mythology (as in the song 'White Mountain'), nature (e.g. 'Stagnation'), religious lyric (e.g. 'Vision of Angels', 'Dusk' and the whole album *From Genesis to Revelation*); 'The Knife' is a protest song
- Visual material: Elaborate surrealistic album covers (cf. the cover of *Trespass*)
- Form: Embellishment of traditional shapes (AABA, verse-chorus), less reliance on traditional shapes; unconventional forms (e.g. the song 'Looking for Someone')

Other elements of this list also fit for Genesis:

- Historical period: Considered 'flourishing' in the early- to mid-1970s
- Historical setting: Originally southern England, especially the London area

- Gender: Primarily male musicians

Also, they used many 'typical' instruments of Progressive Rock: Tony Banks played a "Hammond, [an] battered old electric piano and a mighty twin-manual Mellotron Mk2" (Russell 2004: 20), which especially Steve Hackett was keen on (cf. Russell 2004: 202). Banks is even described as "one of the pioneer users" (Welch 2005: 23) of the Mellotron, notably on the song 'Seven Stones' from their forthcoming album. When looking at their equipment from the 1977 *Wind and Wuthering* tour (cf. Gallo 1978: 152) one can see that they were using many of the instruments that were prominent at the time. Besides the Hammond and the Mellotron, Banks plays an "ARP Pro-Soloist synthesizer" and "not for live shows yet: Roland string synthesizer; ARP 2600 synthesizer; Moog Polymoog; grand piano; etc." Mike Rutherford and Steve Hackett both played, among others, "Fender Stratocaster guitars."

Anthony Phillips played a major part in creating the musical and lyrical features. Unfortunately, he quit the band after the release of *Trespass*, partly because "he had found himself a victim of stage fright" (cf. Thompson 2005: 49). Nowadays he is joking that "the only proof I was ever in the band" is the footage of a concert at the Roundhouse in London in 1970, where they played some songs from *Trespass* (Russell 2004: 12). The band was supporting David Bowie there, who was famous for his costumes onstage, something that would soon be important for Genesis as well. Anthony Phillips would not be in the band to witness it, but he had left remarkable traces, which he would also use in his solo career.

3.1.1 Wise after the event: Anthony Phillips's solo career

Ant Phillips continued writing with Mike Rutherford in the mid-70s, when Genesis had become famous and he was scarcely known for being once in the band (cf. Thompson 2005: 113). People who heard this collaboration told him: 'It sounds like Genesis' (Phillips 2007: 84), something that frustrated him a little bit, especially when the band broke new ground with each album and he was no part of it (cf. Phillips 2007: 85). In 1972, Phil "Collins joined Mike Rutherford and Anthony Phillips in the studio" (Thompson 2005: 105). Collins and Phillips had never been together in Genesis, since Collins joined them after Phillips had left. Phil Collins had not been the singer of Genesis at that time, so it is a little fascinating that the three of them recorded a couple of songs sung by Phil (cf. Platts 2007: 67). It took the record company some time to release them on Phillips' first solo album *The Geese and the ghost* in 1977, a time, when "Phillips quickly came to regret the drummer's involvement", because at that point Collins had taken over the vocals in Genesis, which made "the Genesis comparisons [...] irritating" (Thompson 2005: 139).

The album "did not chart" (Thompson 2005: 139), but Phillips continued to release albums since. Musically he stayed true to himself. He carried on his trademark with "the initial twelve-string guitar material" (Bowler & Dray 1992: 230) and continued to write long and ambitious songs, like the 'Arboretum Suite' (cf. Phillips, A Catch At The Tables). He released another concept album (cf. Phillips, Twelve) and his cover artworks carry on the tradition of being "elaborate" and "surrealistic" (cf. "The Geese and the ghost", "Wise after the event" or "Sides"). His lyrics dealt with religion ("Magdalen"), mythology ("We're All as we lie"), storytelling ("Birdsong") and the simple topic of love ("God if I saw her now").

3.2 And Then There Were Five: 1971-1975

With their next record, the band carried on the elements that should define themselves as well as the genre 'progressive rock' in general. Anthony Phillips was gone and they recruited two new members Phil Collins, who had previously played in a band called Flaming Youth and released one album and a single called 'Guide Me Orion' with them (cf. Waller 1985: 17 f.), and Steve Hackett. Collins was born in 1951 and had a Grammar School and Stage School background, being a working-class kid and thus had a very different background than the other guys in the band (cf. Fielder 1984: 49). He was one of many who answered their ad for a drummer and when he arrived at Peter Gabriel's house he was advised to "have a swim in the private swimming pool", while "the band tried out a couple of other drummers first." He listened to their attempts and afterwards, as Tony Banks says, "he played everything we gave him really perfectly" (Waller 1985: 27).

Hackett, born in 1950 (cf. Fielder 1984: 53), on the other hand, had "placed his ad in *Melody Maker*" (Thompson 2005: 63) and was then called by the group. Both of them brought fresh air into the band, especially Collins with his different attitude and background. Tony Banks (2007: 96) remembers one or the other "violent disagreement" between Gabriel and himself and Collins (2007: 96) understood "that the dynamic I was entering was far more fragile than I had anticipated; [...] Slowly I found that my job became the diffuser of tension."

So, "having given Collins the place at the drum stool" (Bowler & Dray 1992: 40) and after "Hackett's absorption into the group" (Thompson 05: 65) as a new guitarist, they released their third album "*Nursery Cryme* [...] in mid-November 1971" (Thompson 05: 75), with its "stand-out track [...] 'The Musical Box'" (Bowler & Dray 1992: 54). The song was the centrepiece of the album, logically carrying on what they did on *Trespass*.

Apart from this song there were other interesting ground-breaking songs on the album. What struck Hackett when he first heard *Trespass* "was the sound of those beautiful jangling 12-string guitars" (Platts 2007: 40). Based on his own love for acoustic guitar, he wrote the song 'For Absent Friends' which helped "shade Genesis's eventual future" (Thompson 2005: 71), because it was the first "to have Phil singing lead on it." The song "would be positioned between the two epics [...] "The Musical Box" and "The Return of the Giant Hogweed"" (Thompson 2005: 72), two prototype progressive rock songs. 'The Return of the Giant Hogweed' is "about a killer weed that threatens to wipe out mankind" (Bright 1988: 49), and it is "encapsulating both Genesis' dark humour and love of story telling" (Welch 2005: 22). With songs like these, they would move up into the Olympus of progressive rock bands, but the most promising song for that was 'The Musical Box'.

3.2.1   The song 'The Musical Box'

> I know this is sacrilegious to say, but I enjoy Phil singing old Peter Gabriel era songs more than when Petter sang them. This version of Musical Box Closing Section is one of my all time favorite pieces of music. (youtube-user rolabang's comment on the live version from 1977)
>
> SURELY, Surely!!! you jest!!!! Peter Gabriel is a god!!!!!! Phil isn't!!!!!!!!!!!!!!!! (youtube-user angelbabe dawg's reply)

'The Musical Box' is the first song on the "LP's first side" (Thompson 05: 72), written by all members, with lyrics by Peter Gabriel. Anthony Phillips' influence is still very strong on this album, as "parts of the song had been written by Phillips and Rutherford in 1969" (Platts 2007:36). Steve Hackett, on the other hand, did not contribute in writing the song itself, for it was merely finished when he joined the band, but he added some nice guitar effects and elements (cf. Platts 2007: 46). It "received its first major public airing on May 31, 1971, when BBC DJ Bob Harris broadcast a session the band recorded for him three weeks earlier" (Thompson 05: 72) and was played the last time as a whole on *The Lamb Lies Down On Broadway* tour in 1975 (with the exception of a beneficial concert in 1982, where the band reunited with Peter Gabriel to play a set of old songs (cf. Bowler & Dray 92: 181)).

The song is prototypical for the so-called progressive rock genre that emerged during that time. It features a lot of its elements and was one of the reasons why Genesis were seen as major leaders of progressive rock.

The lyrics deal with

> "the story of Henry and Cynthia, two children playing a game of croquet at which Cynthia murders Henry by decapitating him with her mallet. Years later, the dead Henry emerges as an old man from Cynthia's musical box and releases decades of pent-up sexual frustration by raping her" (Holm-Hudson 08: 34).

Peter adds in a live introduction: "The nurse was downstairs however, and she heard strange noises, and rushed up, picked up the musical box, and smashed it into the bearded child destroying both" (Russell 2004: 19). These lyrics evoke "thoughts of nursery rhymes and of *Alice in Wonderland*", which made the song "quintessentially English, placed in the Victorian age" (Bowler & Dray 1992: 55). The song also gave the album its title. The theme also inspired artist Paul Whitehead's sleeve design, which was built "around the imagery of "The Musical Box."" In the sleeve, the story is put in front of the actual lyrics.

Hegarty & Halliwell (2011: 60) think that on the record the "theme of transgression is more specific [...] where it is bounded by a Victorian sense of propriety and normalized morality, symbolized by a well-tended garden." In their opinion it

> "can be read as a countercultural attack on authority, but it is less specific in its social focus than many releases of the late 1960s and does not seek to offer cultural alternatives. Instead, the reader is presented with a series of tangled tales and mythologies that critique respectability but do not provide easy answers."

A live performance of 'The Musical Box' from 1972 was broadcasted on Belgium TV (cf. http://www.youtube.com/watch?v=W35wtfcByIY). Gabriel is dressed completely in black, the other band members are all sitting, almost like in a chamber concert. Steve Hackett (2007: 100) said that "he always thought of himself and the rest of the band sitting down as Peter's pit orchestra." This reminds of the classical influence in progressive rock. In the studio the band is "arranged in their usual shambolic way" with "Banks to the right with his trusty Hammond, battered old electric piano, and a mighty twin-manual Mellotron Mk2", on the left of him "Collins [...] at his smallish drum kit, Gabriel stands behind Collins, whilst Hackett is pushed to the front and hunches over his guitar" and "Rutherford is stage left at the back" (Russell 2004: 20). Apart from 'The Musical Box', they performed 'The Fountain Of Salmacis', 'Twilight Alehouse' and 'The Return Of The Giant Hogweed' at this broadcast (cf. Russell 2004: 20).

The song starts very quietly with Banks and Rutherford playing acoustic guitar and Hackett picking the electric guitar (cf. 00:38), while Gabriel sings and Collins makes some accompanying sounds with tiny chimes and his cymbals (01:01). He gives background vocals to some lines. This passage "had started life in 1969 as the Rutherford/Phillips 12-string demo *F-Sharp*" (Platts 2007: 45). They open the song with their "trademark twelve-string sound" (Bowler & Dray 1992: 55). According to Hegarty & Halliwell (2011: 54) this sound is a "celebration of an English pastoral that inflected one branch of the Anglo-folk tradition rooted in an agrarian version of Olde England, where class-bound loyalties revolve around tales of impossible love and challenges to feudal authority." That would fit exactly to the lyrics of the song. Gabriel sings out of Henry's view from his "half-world" (00:55), he addresses Cynthia and asks her to "play me Old King Cole", so that he can join her (00:12). That refers to the title of the song, the "Musical Box". If she opens it, he will return.

They come to a kind of chorus ("Play me my song..." 01:07), after which they go back into the scheme of the verse (01:19). Gabriel changes between playing his flute and singing (01:25 – 02:47). He begs for "a little bit more time to live out my life." Collins and Gabriel share some harmonies together (01:53). According to Sheinbaum the lyrics of progressive rock often consist of "mythology, modernism" and "surrealism".

Collins starts playing his drums by rolling over the toms; it seems as if the part is finished (02:47 – 03:08). They go back into the chorus ("Play me my song..." 03:08 – 03:22). While the last tones fade out, Banks' organ sets in, changing the atmosphere. Hackett stops picking his guitar and strikes it (03:22). The calmness is over. Collins and Rutherford accompany Hackett's accents, while Banks plays his threatening organ chords in between with some accompanying drums by Collins. It sounds a little bit like a battle between guitar and organ (03:27). Collins sets in and plays thunderous drums to underline the threatening atmosphere of his bandmates (03:40).

The drums set in straight and give a driving beat, Rutherford strums his guitar heavy and Banks keeps playing his chords, while Hackett plays a heavy, but structured guitar solo (03:50 – 04:27). Gabriel hits his tambourine during that passage. Hackett uses the technique of "tapping with the guitar" (Thompson 05: 64), a technique that would later become famous through Eddie Van Halen. Jerry Luck puts "complex arrangements usually featuring intricate keyboard and guitar playing" on his list of elements of progressive rock, something which is very concise here.

After a crescendo, the atmosphere changes all of a sudden. Rutherford strums with an acoustic guitar sound, the drums stop and go back to just light cymbal sounds and Gabriel plays his flute. The danger is over; it seems like a break to breathe deeply, before it goes on. Hackett makes some accompanying sounds, after the flute solo Gabriel and Collins sing in two voices (04:27 – 05:05). Gabriel sings a nursery rhyme about Old King Cole. Cynthia must have opened the musical box, because we hear the nursery rhyme Henry demanded for at the beginning.

On the point, the cymbals stop and we only hear Gabriel's singing and the quiet background noises of Hackett's phasing guitar and Rutherford's acoustic sound (05:05). From then on they become slower and quieter, almost as if the song is at the end (05:05 – 05:20). Henry feels, he touches – he begins to materialize.

With a bang it goes on: Gabriel calls out the last words, the whole band sets in just as in the heavy passage before and Hackett continues with his solo, just as if the part in between was placed into the heavy part and disrupted everything. He takes turns with Banks, who plays some short solos on the organ. The battle goes on (05:20 – 06:34). At this point, it builds "up to a powerful instrumental climax, mirroring Henry's desires" with "Steve and Tony combining superbly above an invigorated rhythm section" (Bowler & Dray 1992: 55). The song consists "a mixture of loud passages, soft passages, and musical crescendos to add to the dynamics of the arrangements" which is another element of progressive rock.

After that, they go back to the threatening scheme before the heavy parts, as if playing the song backwards (06:34). The part ends with as bang as it began (07:06). The transformation is over. Henry has returned and during this heavy part, he went through all the stages of his life up to the point of being an old man. One might assume that the chords of the very first part might follow now, but they are not. The "embellishment of traditional shapes (AABA, verse-chorus)" and "less reliance on traditional shapes" are classic progressive rock elements.

It does become quiet again and we only hear plucked guitar. This is the most famous section of the song. Tony Banks (07: 107) remembers its genesis, "where Mike had this little chord sequence and I started playing these very simple major chords on top of it so that it became almost like a fugue, quiet quietly, before developing into something that was really, really exciting." With this the band was creating another of progressive rock's trademark, as "a handful of groups could be said to be intent on emulating [...] classical music" (Hegarty & Halliwell 2011: 12).

Gabriel sings. Collins provides backing vocals, singing against Gabriel's line (07:13 – 07:39). Henry sees Cynthia and he demands her. He wants to see her face. The story was "dramatized by the old-man costume worn by Gabriel for live performances in 1972" (Hegarty & Halliwell 2011: 60). After one verse, it is repeated, the lyrics and the singing become a little more threatening (07:39). His desire grows – he demands her flesh instead of her face. The organ sets in, very pastoral, very majestic. Together with the cymbals of Collins and Gabriel's vocals, one hears that it slowly leads to a climax (07:58). The same passage repeats itself, even more suspenseful. Gabriel yells at Cynthia and asks her to touch him (08:58 – 08:42). The whole passage is built up like an orgasm, reaching the climax: Organ, drums, and guitars all play heavy punctuated accents. Gabriel just screams the words "Now!" with the accents (08:42 – 09:10). In the lyrics, Gabriel describes an "exploration of sexual undercurrents in society" (Holm-Hudson 08: 36).

The orgasm is over. Gabriel stops singing, the band plays straight and full again, Hackett plays a guitar solo (09:10 – 09:26). Heavy accents by the band, then chaos and the last blow. Song is over (09:26 – 09:36). Henry gets killed by the nurse. It was a "Nursery Crime". With its length of about 10 minutes, Genesis are using another of progressive rock's elements, which describes "songs predominantly on the longish side, but structured, rarely improvised".

It was the first time on a live performance of that song, that Peter Gabriel "started dressing up in all manner of things" (Hackett 07: 124). In general, it began when he "shaved the top of his head" (Fielder 1984: 60). After the release of their next album *Foxtrot*, which "came out in October 1972" (Bowler & Dray 1992: 69), Gabriel, who "was blessed with the gift of being able to hold an audience in the palm of his hand, coupled with the sensibility never to abuse that power" (Bowler & Dray 1992: 48) appeared onstage for 'The Musical Box' with "a long red dress [...] and a fox head" (Bowler & Dray 1992: 70) in style of the *Foxtrot* cover and sang the end of 'The Musical Box'. The band was surprised for Gabriel did not inaugurate them (cf. Russell 2004: 33), but the "fox's head was on the front page of *Melody Maker* the following week" as Tony Banks (2007: 124) remembers: "We had difficult music to get across [...] You need something more than just music to attract a bigger audience." The costumes became one of Gabriel's trademarks in Genesis and he shaped the presentation of progressive rock music as well. It started with "Ian Anderson's bizarre stage persona of eccentric tramp-cum-minstrel with unkempt hair and dressed in a long coat [...] and foreshadowed the emphasis on theatricality in the performances of Yes, Genesis and Rush in the mid-1970s" (Hegarty & Halliwell 2011: 51). And Ed Goodgold, the band's promoter in the United States, compared Peter Gabriel to a priest and his costumes to his vestments (cf. Goodgold in Banks et al. 2007: 130). Russell (2004: 39) also thinks that, when for example he was wearing "a shiny silver outfit" for 'The Return of the Giant Hogweed', where "Genesis rock out" and "the crowd are on their feet", "Gabriel continues to steal the show." In this aspect, Gabriel has also often been compared with Alice Cooper and David Bowie (cf. Holm-Hudson, 2008: 30). It is also important to note that the band in the beginning did not intend to play their songs live, but rather that "other artists would record them" (Platts 2007: 11). Gabriel's costumes were a way of presenting the songs for the audience, as the young, shy public school boys were actually not the most natural performers onstage. He hid himself behind theses masks and became someone different.

From 1973 onwards, Gabriel used a special costume for 'The Musical Box'. Peter Gabriel "became" Henry, slipping backstage during an extended instrumental passage and then emerged with "a disturbing malevolent old-man mask, miming Henry's sexual climax" (Bowler & Dray 1992: 75). He was "living and breathing the part of Henry; desperation, lust, frustration all communicated in a vocal *tour de force*" (Bowler & Dray 1992: 55).

'The Musical Box' resembles all the features of progressive rock. It is a classic prototype of a progressive rock song. Gabriel's lyrics were "accompanied by the strongest music that Genesis had yet put on record" (Bowler & Dray 1992: 55). Of course, Genesis was one of the bands that invented those typical elements of progressive rock. Songs like 'The Musical Box' were used as blue-print for the characteristics of the genre. Not considering all these theoretical elements for a moment one can simply say that the song still "stands today as a potent, emotional piece of music" (Bowler & Dray 1992: 55). Since Anthony Phillips' sound is still very strongly integrated, Phil Collins' influence would only grow much later and Steve Hackett was only partly integrated in the making of this song, the band's very British background is still reflected in the song and the lyrics.

In later years, the band only played the last passage of the song (cf. http://www.youtube.com/watch?v=Ap-6KLzdfFI). Phil Collins has been heavily criticized when singing the Peter Gabriel songs, which is a stark contrast to the fact that the fans always wanted to hear the old songs (details in the chapter "The song 'Abacab'"). Thompson (2005: 133) says that listening to "Gabriel's version of "The Musical Box" [...] is simply spellbinding", whereas "Collins, performing the same song, scarcely even seemed aware of it", although the music, the musicians and the lyrics are the same and the costume was replaced by a light show (cf. 01:45) for the visual effect.

Anyway, back in 1972, the next big step was yet about to come. On the already mentioned next album *Foxtrot*, they reached their "progressive" high-point with...

3.2.2   The song 'Supper's ready'

> Gabriel said that Collins did a better version. Well Gabriel is really so humble. Phil never can sing as Gabriel. Neither in a million years (youtube-user Michael Paul McCartney's comment on the live-version from 1973)

> Dislike. Sorry, I tried to keep an open mind but I just can't get into Genesis without Peter Gabriel. (youtube-user TheRabidPosum's comment on the live version from 1976)

'Supper's Ready' was "the centrepiece of the album" and "took up almost all of the second side" (Bowler & Dray 1992: 65). The only other song, right before it, is "'Horizons' a short but nonetheless attractive Steve Hackett solo acoustic pieces, with some nifty harmonics" (Welch 2005: 27 ff.), with which Hackett held up Ant Phillips's flag. 'Supper's ready' itself

> "is sub-divided as follows: (1) Lovers' Leap, (2) The Guaranteed Eternal Sanctuary Man, (3) Ikhnaton And Itsacon and Their Band Of Merry Men (4) How Dare I Be So Beautiful? (5) Willow Farm (6) Apocalypse In 9/8 (Co-Starring The Delicious Talents Of Gabble Ratchet) and (7) As Sure As Eggs Is Eggs (Aching Men's Feet)" (Welch 2005: 27 ff.).

It is "a collection of short songs, connected by musical bridge passages and a strong lyrical theme" as Bowler & Dray (1992: 65) explain it and they compare it to "classical suites [that] are made up of shorter sections which together create one flowing movement." As for the features of progressive rock, it is to mention that Jerry Luck gives the song as an example for all the features on his list of progressive rock elements. And just as the song 'The Musical Box' served as an inspiration for the cover of *Nursery Cryme,* Paul "Whitehead's cover painting for FOXTROT was largely inspired by *Supper's Ready*" (Platts 2007: 56).

To this day, ""Supper's Ready" remains one of Genesis's best-loved and best-executed vinyl performances, and it was destined to make an immediate impression in concert as well" (Thompson 2005: 84), which can be seen in this live version from 1973: http://www.youtube.com/watch?v=M58wE8GTGp4.

Gabriel is dressed completely in black, wearing white make-up. His

"use of grease paint from 1970 onwards (during and beyond his time as lead singer of Genesis) to create an odd cast of characters was linked to a fondness for bizarre costumes set against abstract stage sets, through which Gabriel became a character in the song or morphed into a mythical figure" (Hegarty & Halliwell 2011: 122).

He makes an introduction (00:15 – 02:33), something that was also characteristically for him (cf. Russell 2004: 18). He explains that "the storytelling had emerged as a means of filling in the gaps when we had thirty-six strings being tuned by people who weren't very good at tuning them" (Gabriel 2007: 113). At 01:50, he uses Phil Collins as sideman, who explains: "I became his stooge" (Collins 2007: 113).

02:41: 'Lover's Leap' starts, where "a 12-string guitar plays a beautiful melody to create a romantic mood" (Welch 2005: 28). In fact Banks, Hackett and Rutherford all play acoustic guitar and Banks (2007: 121) explained that this intro "had started off acoustically, like 'Stagnation' and 'Musical Box'", where they also all played guitar. Gabriel sings the lyrics, which "came from an experience that he and [his wife at that time] Jill had" (Bowler & Dray 1992: 66). A friend of theirs "was very interested in spiritualism and had been talking to Jill at length about the subject and the idea of power and strength of will when the atmosphere in the room changed dramatically, Jill going into a trance as the windows blew open" (Bowler & Dray 1992: 67) and Peter said that "We saw other faces in each other. It was almost as if something else had come into us and was using us as a meeting point" (Bright 1988: 51).

He sings from 02:41 – 03:11 "of a couple sitting in a front room who switch off the television and listen to the sound of traffic" (Hegarty & Halliwell 2011: 97) before he comes to the 'chorus' with its soulful cry of "Hey baby, don't you know our love is true"" (Welch 2005: 28). At 03:36 the verse is repeated, the storyteller sees "six shrouded figures that materialize in the garden and presage a dreamlike world into which [he] falls into a series of visions" (Hegarty & Halliwell 2011: 97). The chorus comes again (04:07), in which "they have doubts about whether their love for each other is true, or if the beloved 'guardian eyes so blue' can offer adequate protection from the unknown" (Hegarty & Halliwell 2011: 97). This is a reflection of Gabriel's experience with his wife. At 04:40 the "acoustic guitars beaver away, then an electric piano joins in the fun as the *danse macabre* begins" as Welch (2005: 28) calls it, and then "Peter breathes a lover's greeting: "It's been a long time. Hasn't it" with gentle understatement."

At 07:17 "the band finally make their appearance on 'Sanctuary Man'" (Welch 2005: 27 ff.). Peter wears a crown of thorns, lyrically he "referenced the Bible" in "an epic tale of good versus evil" (Platts 2007: 56). Musically, this whole passage "was composed by Banks around the time he started university" (Thompson 2005: 85). The band gets quiet, the mood changes at 08:25, as "there is pause for thought and reflection" and "Children's voice chant a nursery rhyme during 'Sanctuary Man'" (Welch 2005: 28). The "'Sanctuary Man' cannot distract the quester from scenes of war in which 'the children of the west' (09:06) and 'a host of dark skinned warriors' (09:12) wait for battle" (Hegarty & Halliwell 2011: 97). At 09:25 the whole band sets in again and "Peter heralds a clash of dark forces." Welch (2005: 28) compares the action of the lyrics with the action of the band: ""Killing for peace…bang, bang, bang!" he [Peter] yells as the combined forces of Hackett, Rutherford, Banks and Collins march into action" (09:42). Hackett plays a guitar solo from 10:13 onwards up to 10:50, where "a sudden halt creates a cliff hanging moment for tension before the main riff is repeated" (Welch 2005: 28). Peter sings again, the "battle between civilization and savagery ends in jubilation, where dancing and rejoicing suggest a change of order" (Hegarty & Halliwell 2011: 97) from 11:17 – 11:38.

The band becomes quiet again, until there is only Tony Banks playing very slowly (12:02 – 12:21). Welch (2005: 28) praises "Gabriel's gift of extracting maximum meaning and sensual effect from well chosen words […] on 'How Dare I Be So Beautiful?' when in the aftermath of battle he says: "We climb up the mountain of human *flesh*"" (12:40), which the storyteller has "to climb in order to achieve a higher perspective […] and he bemoans the enslavement of survivors who have been 'stamped human bacon by some butchery tool.' (13:04)" Instead of "an extended critique of the battle or a moral assessment of the loss of life" (Hegarty & Halliwell 2011: 97), "the final line of this piece "…Narcissus is turned to a flower," concludes with "A Flower?"" at 13:34 and brings "some light relief"

(Russell 2004: 60) into the performance. Gabriel appears "with a huge flower wreathing his head" (Welch 2005: 28), which "became one of the most recognizable Gabriel costumes of the period" (Platts 2007: 61).

The band goes "into an absurdist section" (Hegarty & Halliwell 2011: 97), a "distinct song that Peter had written on piano called 'Willow Farm'" (Banks 2007: 121). It was Banks' suggestion "that after every romantic acoustic passage they should just stop the song and launch into a new one." The song is "a real oddity, filled with clever wordplay and imagery" (Bowler & Dray 1992: 66). Welch (2005: 28) sees Gabriel as "growing ever more surreal" as at 13:48 he "appeared dancing in tight black trousers [and] chants over a suitably silly march, "There's Winston Churchill dressed in drag, he used to be a British flag, plastic bag...what a drag" (14:20)" and sees "this piece of eccentric nonsense [...] much in the tradition of Edward Lear and John Lennon."

Steve Hackett (in Thompson 2005: 85) sees 'Willow Farm' "as one of my favourites" and agrees that "it was Beatlesque, very catchy. I thought that was the band playing at its best. Because it was pastiche, it was possible to do that with gusto in most situations." Bowler & Dray (1992: 67) describe "the inclusion of 'Willow Farm'" together with Gabriel's performance as a "theatre of the absurd."

At 15:12 the band "stops in its tracks with a cry of "All change!"" (Welch 2005: 28). Gabriel (in Platts 2007: 56) linked 'Willow Farm' with the album cover, which

> "originally [...] was going to be a fox on an ice cube, [...] and then Steve and I wanted it to be a fox changing into a woman because we're both attracted just by the idea of a change, really. That's what *Willow Farm* is about in that it's a sort of Zen farm where the only thing that is constant is a stage of change, which probably has a neutralizing effect in itself."

Gabriel even thought of creating his own 'Willow Farm' or 'Real World Experience', by buying

> "a hundred-acre farm in North Wales and turn it into a cross between Disneyland and an art gallery, where the visitor goes through a tremendous amount of first hand experiences which would completely upturn his points of relativity and put him through a series of changes."

According to Hegarty & Halliwell (2011: 97) Gabriel sings about "biological transfiguration" ('feel your body melt' 15:13) and as they finish 'Willow Farm' with the words 'end with a whistle, or end with a bang' (16:10) about "eschatological sense of finitude." In this line he wordplays again and "parodies the last line of T.S. Eliot's 1925 poem 'The Hollow Men.'"

The next part (at 16:18), "'Apocalypse' begins with doomy chords, heralding an Elizabethan style serenade on flute and guitar" (Welch 2005: 28). The next battle is about to come (18:23), this time "between the mythical giants Gog and Magog" (Hegarty & Halliwell 2011: 97). What follows is "the finest piece of music that Genesis have ever written and performed, 'Apocalypse In 9/8' and the closing 'Aching Men's Feet' [...] born out of improvisation by Mike, Tony and Phil" (Bowler & Dray 1992: 66). Rutherford (2007: 121) sees this as the "start of what was later going to be the three-piece unit." Creating this part proofs that "even before Hackett and Gabriel left the group, Collins, Rutherford and Banks seemed to form the musical core of Genesis, sharing an intuitive musical communication with each other" (Platts 2007: 46).

The passage begins at 19:00 and consists of "a grinding, angular organ solo over a pounding, relentless rhythm in 9/8" (Welch 2005: 66) created by Rutherford and Collins. Banks (2007: 122) "took it as a 4/4 thing and played right against their riff." Russell (2004: 60) describes the atmosphere onstage as "a flame engulfed battlesfield, the lightning against the gauze sails give the impression of flickering flames." As the passage rolls on, "Phil's drums skitter around the Hammond as Tony's stabbing notes become increasingly hysterical during a lengthy instrumental interlude" (Welch 2005: 28) and at the end of the solo, "when Pete suddenly started singing [...] – '666' – [at 21:36] it takes it onto another level" (Banks 2007: 122).

Gabriel appears on stage with "a strange box mask for the '666' section" (Bowler & Dray 1992: 75). He sings at 21:55 that the battle "of evil and good rage deep 'down inside your soul'" (Hegarty & Halliwell 2011: 97). A picture of this scene would appear on the album *Genesis Live* from 1973 and Russell (2004: 60) thinks "this is rock theatre at its peak."

At 22:50 "bells chime and the snare drum rolls as Gabriel sounds a return to the theme from 'Lover's Leap'" (Welch 2005: 28). The "black cloak that [...] was torn off in a flash of light to reveal Peter in a shining white suit (23:05)" represents "the final triumph of good over evil" (Bowler & Dray 1992: 75). The lyrics repeat from 'Lover's Leap', and "we are reintroduced to the lover" (23:20) and "the confidence that things will work out 'fine' (23:35) links closely to natural processes ('how the river joins the ocean' 24:05)" (Hegarty & Halliwell 2011: 97). Welch (2005: 28) explains that

> "the dénouement of this massive work is reached with 'As Sure As Eggs Is Eggs', where the tempo reverts to a slow but steady rock beat, with huge

notes from Mike Rutherford's bass pedals underpinning an exultant guitar rhythm. It sounds like the whole band is waving farewell." (23:20 – 25:41)

Bowler & Dray (1992: 75) think that the song was a "sufficient proof for some that Genesis were dull, pretentious prog-rockers", whereas they think that "Genesis proved themselves to be light years apart from the progressive rockers with whom they were clumsily classified" because as Mike Rutherford said in an interview with BBC Scotland, "even on a song of this length, 'we were simple and melodic.'"

Hegarty & Halliwell (2011: 9) agree that

> "it is undeniable that many progressive rock musicians, especially in the 1970s, were talented, skilful and creative. The question is whether this hindered or helped musical creativity, particularly as progressive bands were interested in different ways of writing and performing as a group and of developing ideas into integrated concept albums, rather than filling out albums and concerts with tracks featuring virtuoso solos."

Lyrically, there are different interpretations and many tried to work it out. It is clear that they "were the brainchild of Gabriel" and that it is "an epic tale of good versus evil that referenced the Bible, Winston Churchill, Greek mythology and, indirectly, Jonathan King ("How dare I be so beautiful?" was a King catch phrase)" (Platts 2007: 56). They also refer to the band themselves ("And the musical box", 14:08) and include another nursery rhyme at 08:25. In 'Willow Farm' they "celebrate this same Englishness" (Holm-Hudson 2008: 26) as in 'The Musical Box'.

Kevin Holm-Hudson (2008: 125) sees the lyrics as "a Gabrielesque vision of the battle of Armageddon and the second coming of Christ" and Chris Welch (2005: 28) thinks that it "explores the complexities of human relationships, the threat of external forces and the ultimate power of love to heal." Steve Hackett himself admits (in Thompson 2005: 85) that "lyrically, you couldn't really pin it down. There was the gobbledygook factor and all the rest, and in the middle of this long piece, you had the mini-pop songs." Reflecting on the whole song he says that "the word Elgar comes to mind for some reason, Elgar on acid perhaps" (Hackett 2007: 123). Edward Elgar is one of the "composers of the so-called 'English Renaissance'" (Mackerness 1964: 210 f.). He "is thought of as a very 'English' composer", being famous for "the patriotic *Land of Hope and Glory*" (Room 1990: 113). The comparison to him underlines the "Englishness" of 'Supper's Ready'.

However one may interpret the lyrics, Bowler & Dray (1992: 75) think that "Genesis did not over-reach themselves" and that "it is to Genesis' credit that [the lyric] was treated with great subtlety allied to a nice line in cynicism" (Bowler & Dray 1992: 67). Thompson (2005: 84) thinks that the track "would sum up every facet of the band's abilities and interests" and quotes Steve Hackett, who says

> "when we first wrote that, and performed it live, I really thought that the game was up and we'd be sussed for the imposters we were. [...] The reverse was true. We were hailed as beings from another realm, that managed to come up with this magic stuff, and so my instincts were entirely wrong."

And Richard MacPhail (in Banks et al 2007: 111), their road manager in the 1970s and a close friend of the band thinks that 'Supper's Ready' "was as far as I was concerned was the greatest piece of music ever written."

The song was often performed live in the following years. A live video of the second half of the song with Phil Collins as a frontman shows the different approaches of him and Gabriel. It was played in 1976 (http://www.youtube.com/watch?v=0FrFytItybk) with Bill Bruford on drums, whom they hired for this one tour and who among others "played with Yes and King Crimson" (Platts 2007: 86). Welch (2005: 85) is of the opinion that "although held to be a better recording than the original, this is an oddly flat version of the *Foxtrot* album classic."

The band starts at 00:02 with 'Apocalypse in 9/8', the flute part being played by the piano. At 01:01 we hear Collins sing. Welch (2005: 85) admits that "Phil does his best, but he isn't Peter Gabriel, and Peter's manic intensity and propensity for the bizarre is sorely missed." The missing costumes are replaced by the lights which reflect Phil (01:01, 04:27). The rest of the band does not get Welch's full credit, too, as he writes that "there is some good playing of course, notably from Tony Banks who offers dynamic organ work (01:45), and 'Apocalypse In 9/8' is brightened by snare drum exchanges" by the two drummers (01:53). Bill Bruford (in Banks et al 2007: 198) admits that "it is quite possible that I caused irritation, because my nature is to play a piece differently every night even though there are only so many ways you can play 'Supper's Ready' on a drum kit without the song unravelling." According to Welch "there is no guts to the performance" and in his view, "'Supper's Ready' sounds microwaved rather than oven cooked" (Welch 2005: 85 f.). The film sequences that are seen were added to the video afterwards, they were not part of the concert, although they fit well to the song and make up for the absence of the costumes. Thompson (2005: 133) thinks that Collins "was never going to make [...] "Supper's Ready" his own." But that was never what he intended to. He knew he was not Peter and describes the song as "a task he dreaded" (Thompson 2005: 134). Nevertheless the band decided to play this song which was very much part of Peter Gabriel (who actually did not play the song himself anymore after he had left the band; cf. Holm-Hudson 2008: 64). Whether one likes it or not, one has to admit that the band sounds great and Phil sings the songs with light and clear voice. Funnily enough, when Collins was on his first solo tour with his own band in 1982, "a contingent of Genesis die-hards inevitably turned up at Collins' solo dates and there were a few cries for *Supper's Ready*, to which he responded with an abridged, 10-second rendition: 'A flower?...Six six six...Jerusalem...'" (Platts 2007: 127)

Although 'Supper's Ready' was the masterpiece of *Foxtrot*, there were "other songs that [...] were not dwarfed by its presence" (Bowler & Dray 1992: 67). The other highlight was another prototypical prog-song, 'Watcher of the Skies'. The song features "an imaginative sci-fi lyric by Mike and Tony" about "the Mysterious One, contemplating the fate of a departed human race" (Welch 2005: 26). It is known for its "towering adagio mellotron introduction" (Bowler & Dray 1992: 67). When performed live, Peter Gabriel played the "Watcher of The Skies", wearing "batwings" on his head and glaring "at the audience with luminous eyes" (Welch 2005: 26).

The song was also one of the band's attempts to reach a chart position with a single, but it failed. I will talk about it in more detail in a later chapter, but it should be noted that the band at this point in time tried to have hits. When they reached this aim in later years, they were blamed for it. Ironically, a favourite of many fans was the song 'I Know What I Like' from their next album *Selling England by the Pound*, which was the first time they charted with a single.

3.2.3 The song 'I Know What I Like (In Your Wardrobe)'

I appreciate Phil Collins, but in this song his vocal can't measure with Peter Gabriel. (youtube-user Evergreen Best Music's comment on the live version from 1976)

This is the best version of this song. I'd like to see Tool cover it... (youtube-user 90th Meridian's comment on the live version from 1976)

With their previous albums, Genesis had marked themselves as one of the ultimate prog-rock bands. They had found their style that was characteristic for them in this line-up. *Selling England by the Pound*, when given to their record company's manager Tony Stratton-Smith was the first album "he didn't seem that excited by what they had given him" (Welch 2005: 31).

The band again produced some typical progressive songs, like 'The Cinema Show', which according to Collins "has very elaborated arrangement and is played in seven" (Thompson 2005: 102). Indeed "the very strong instrumental section at the end of 'The Cinema Show'" was "another long improvisation session between Mike, Tony and Phil" (Bowler & Dray 1992: 79). Peter Gabriel even "fought to excise the closing instrumental passage of "The Cinema Show" – moments that would, once the album was released, be singled out among the most evocative on the entire record" (Thompson 2005: 102). And Steve Hackett "freely admits that following *Foxtrot* he wanted to approach *Selling England* purely as a player, with no great interest in writing, 'Yet I ended up writing a couple of key things for the band'" for "he contributed an emotionally charged solo, which many still regard as the crowning moment of his time with the band", (Bowler & Dray 1992: 81) on the song 'Firth Of Fifth'.

The length of most of the songs also was as long as ever, for songs like ""The Battle of Epping Forest" and "The Cinema Show" both clocked in at more than 11 minutes" (Thompson 2005: 102). 'The Cinema Show' fades into 'Aisle of Plenty', a song that repeats musical themes from the first song on the album, 'Dancing With The Moonlit Knight', "a piece that seems to mourn the passing of some mythical England as the country enters into the commercialised, strife torn world of the uncertain Seventies" (Welch 2005: 31). The song "was still full of stories and character portraits", just like 'The Battle of Epping Forest', and 'I Know What I Like', which were, according to Hackett (2007: 148), "still very English." These characters were of course played onstage by Gabriel. For 'The Battle of Epping Forest' he "would often war a stocking on his head" (Russell 2004: 53) and for 'Dancing with the Moonlit Knight' he would play "Britannia" (Russell 2004: 59). Britannia is "a personification of Great Britain on coins, etc in the form of a seated woman holding a trident in one hand and wearing a helmet" (Room 1990: 42).

With 'I Know What I Like (In Your Wardrobe)' they had "their first British hit" (Holm-Hudson 2008: 45). It was based on "another riff of Steve" which "had been around since *Foxtrot*, but everyone thought it sounded too much like the Beatles", as he says and he continues: "I kept playing it and finally everyone else joined in and it became our first hit single – no one else has ever said that it sounds like the Beatles!'" (Bowler & Dray 1992: 79)

Tony Banks (Russell 2004: 207) liked "the simplicity of "I Know What I Like"" and indeed the song was moving on a different territory than their previous long, elaborate songs. It led the band into new areas, which would lead to their harshly criticized single success in the following decades. Still, this song is described by Thompson (2005: 107) as "a masterpiece, tight and concise."

Of course, Gabriel dressed up for the song on live versions. In this version (cf. http://www.youtube.com/watch?v=Za6DWVasjTw) from a TV studio in 1974 we can see him in make-up and wearing a hat, being described by Russell (2004: 83) as looking "like a WW1 German soldier's helmet." He is playing the "human lawnmower", the storyteller of the song and he pretends to mow the lawn to the sounds of the keyboards (00:04), which create "strange whining noises like helicopter" (Welch 2005: 32).

At 00:47 "a light-hearted spoken word intro" (Thompson 2005: 107) begins ("It's one o'clock and time for lunch...") and afterwards (00:59) the songs leaps into "the band's first straight ahead pop rock song" (Welch 2005: 32).

The verse is carried by "a spellbinding Steve Hackett guitar riff" (Thompson 2005: 107) and Gabriel adopts "various personae" and according to Holm-Hudson (2008: 36) the song can be seen "as a miniature monodrama in which Gabriel "acts out" all of the parts." The chorus sets in at 01:26 and Phil Collins, who "contributed backing vocals on the chorus", helps Peter out with the different characters. Thompson (2005: 107) thinks of it as "a chorus that you could swing through trees on."

After a funny interlude from 01:57 – 02:08, the verse sets in again "with a stomping, steady beat and hook lines galore." Its lyrics are typical for Gabriel, being "rich in imagery and full of comic surprises." The lyrics were "inspired by the Betty Swanwick painting that graced the album sleeve" (Platts 2007: 65). The verse runs until 02:32 and reaches the "chanted chorus, where Gabriel and Collins combine" (Welch 2005: 32). The chorus is repeated at 02:57 up until 03:30, when this time "a light-hearted spoken word outro" (Thompson 2005: 107) follows ("Me – I'm just a lawn mower. You can tell me by the way I walk."). The song ends with a bit of flute-playing over the strange keyboard noises that the song began with. Then Gabriel acts out the lawnmower and this is it. A short pop number, only about five minutes. That was the reason why "Charisma first mooted "I Know What I Like (In Your Wardrobe)" as a single in late 1973 to coincide with the release of *Selling England by the Pound*" (Thompson 2005: 107).

Funnily enough, the fans "loved it" and "were mostly delighted to see them gain public recognition" (Welch 2005: 32) as it reached "#21 in the British charts, with the FOXTROT outtake *Twilight Alehouse* on its flip side" (Platts 2007: 67). Mike Rutherford (2007: 145) says, that "people always said we started going for singles in the 1980s. We'd made singles for years. It was just that they were crap." When the band was offered that footage from the Shepperton Film Studios could be "intended to promote the single" (Russell 2004: 60) by being shown on 'Top of the Pops', they refused the offer!

Interestingly, the band stretched out this song live when Phil Collins took over the microphone, making it much more "progressive" than the original "pop" version. In a live version from 1976 (http://www.youtube.com/watch?v=eK9a2jLEAfs) from the band's first tour without Peter Gabriel, Phil Collins sings the song. The drums are played by Bill Bruford.

The length of this version is 06:21. The drums set in very early at 00:12 over the organ sounds from Tony Banks. The guitar plays some sound effects from 00:29 onwards. Phil Collins starts singing at 00:46 and at 00:56 the verse starts. The band sounds "fuller" than in 1974 and Welch (2005: 84) praises "Phil's 'scat' singing" as "one of the highlight of this extended version of their early hit song." At 01:21 the chorus begins. It does not sound that different to the original version, mainly because Phil sang background vocals on it and was very prominent. The song goes along as usual and the second chorus (02:21) becomes a sing-a-long for the whole band, while Rutherford and Collins joke around, singing into one microphone like The Beatles used to do it in their early days and by this pointing out the Beatlesque style that Steve Hackett mentioned.

Instead of ending the song after the verse, from 03:11 onwards Phil "does his tambourine routine [...] drawing roars of applause" (Welch 2005: 85). It was to become one of Phil's trademarks and he did it on all live versions of the song until 2007. After the spoken words (04:02) an extended outro is played, causing Welch (2005: 85) to say that "the piece actually starts to fall asleep during a long, coasting instrumental section." The section is characterized by Phil playing also the drums and the percussions, Hackett playing around on the guitar and "Mike Rutherford's nifty bass patterns" that "provide some of the most interesting moments" (Welch 2005: 85). Tony Banks plays a melody from 'Stagnation' (05:16) from their second album *Trespass*. At 05:41 they play one last chorus, the point where according to Welch (2005: 85) the piece "wakes up on its return to the theme." The song ends at 06:21.

The two versions both bear the trademarks of each singer. Whereas Gabriel acts out his role alone and the focus is just on him, Collins integrates the whole band by putting hats on their heads and makes fun with the tambourine or plays the drums. The whole band plays tighter and better and the whole song gets a "progressive" touch in the instrumental section (especially with progressive-rock drummer Bill Bruford), something that is missed on the original version. But then again, on *Selling England By The Pound* there is the song 'More Fool Me', "written by Mike Rutherford and Phil Collins", who also "takes the vocal here", being called by Welch (2005: 32) "the most effective item on the album" as it "foreshadows Collins's future solo career."

3.2.4 The album The Lamb Lies Down On Broadway

> In My Honest Opinion, This was and still the best Genesis Album of The Progressive Rock Era(1969-1977)!!!!!! (youtube-user Cameron Graham's comment on the video of the album)

> Like "The Wall" it has a lot of musical highlights but the "concept" isn't much to speak of, somewhere between banal and pompous most of the time. Another word that comes to mind is "bloated" . . . a bloated lamb? lol (youtube-user OroborusFMA's comment on the video of the album)

Their next album should be the last album with Peter Gabriel. They wrote it at "Headley Grange, a manor house in Hampshire" (Holm-Hudson 2008: 49), which was used by the likes of Led Zeppelin. The album was named *The Lamb Lies down on Broadway* and it was their "most ambitious work" (Welch 2005: 34). It is "a double concept LP" (Welch 2005: 35) and "is – along with the 26-minute epic "Supper's Ready" – regarded as the apex of Genesis's progressive ambitions" (Holm-Hudson 2008: 133). Because of that and because of the "complicated, demanding story line, developed by Peter Gabriel" (Welch 2005: 34), which was the subject of analysis for many writers, I will not go into too much detail and write about every song (there is a book which deals with an analysis of the whole album), but will give a short overview and point out some Genesis trademarks in some of the songs. The whole album can be found here: https://www.youtube.com/watch?v=MRSgvfNZcWA

On the previous albums Genesis had marked their style and people expected certain things from their band. The band knew that, but "Gabriel's comic fantasy stories that had so endeared him to fans lost their appeal when taken too seriously and spread over four sides of an album" (Welch 2005: 34). Welch sums up that "across some 23 tracks Gabriel told the story of Rael, the spray gun toting Puerto Rican punk from New York City." Rael is sucked "into a netherworld" and goes through a story that "is dreamlike, held together by a double quest to escape [...] and for self-awareness" (Hegarty & Halliwell 2012: 77). Next to Rael, there are some other "strange visitors to an increasingly overcrowded Broadway" as Welch (2005: 40) calls it. Among the different characters, there are the so-called Slippermen, the Lamia ("crucial figures to the tale, with their heads and breasts of beautiful women who live in an ornate pink water pool") or the "supernatural anaesthetist", who "is death personified" (Welch 2005: 39).

This story was "a decisive break from their earlier image of myth and fantasy" (Holm-Hudson 2008: 56), being "full of references to contemporary American figures" and it was "a radical departure for Peter to attempt a theme set far away from his beloved England" (Welch 2005: 34). Previous to the album, the band had toured North America and were trying to become successful in the United States (cf. Platts 2007: 68). It was also (after the failed attempt on their first record) their first real "concept album", which "was a beloved format for progressive rock groups" (Holm-Hudson 2008: 46). They barely wrote the album together, as "Gabriel busied himself with the story" and "his bandmates turned their attention to setting it all to the music" (Thompson 2005: 114). Only the lyrics for one song, 'The Light Dies Down On Broadway', "were written not by Gabriel, but by Banks and Rutherford" (Holm-Hudson 2008: 92). This split-up way of working caused that many "songs on the album came about from improvisations" (Holm-Hudson 2008: 59) between Banks, Collins and Rutherford, while Hackett describes his role on *The Lamb* as "an innocent bystander" (Fielder 1984: 92). According to Chris Welch (2005: 40) songs like 'Hairless Heart' (28:44 – 30:56) or 'Here comes the supernatural anaesthetist' (56:59 – 59:45) show "how Steve could have galvanised the whole *Lamb* concept if the lead guitar had been given a little more space." There were also some other differences between Gabriel and the rest of the band that overshadowed the making of the album. For one, "William Friedkin, who directed *The Exorcist*" (Bright 1988: 59) had read Gabriel's story "on the back of the *Genesis Live* record" (Gabriel 2007: 151) and "asked if he was interested in writing a film script" (Bright 1988: 59). Gabriel was interested, but "Friedkin backed away when he realized he could be responsible for splitting the band" (Bright 1988: 59). The other thing was that "Jill was pregnant with our first child" and "when Anna was born in July '74 there were all sorts of complications" (Gabriel 2007: 154). Gabriel started to alienate from the band during that time, something that is reflected in the story of *The Lamb Lies Down On Broadway*.

In the title track (00:00 – 04:52) the story of "Rael, [the] half Puerto Rican" (Holm-Hudson 2008: 65) begins. Its "main theme provides some of the most memorable moments from the whole enterprise, and it was to survive in the band's set for years to come" (Welch 2005: 36). The song was one of only two Genesis songs that were played live by "Peter Gabriel, in his early career as a solo artist" (Holm-Hudson 2008: 64). The song starts with "Tony Banks' rhapsodic piano introduction" (00:00), before "Hackett and Collins drive proceedings forward (00:32), adding to the sense of urgency as Peter sets the scene with emphatic vocals (00:52)" (Welch 2005: 36). The song is "an energetic rock number dominated by a distinctive bass riff (cf. 01:21) by Mike Rutherford" (Holm-Hudson 2008: 63). The song follows a simple scheme, it "relies more on expanded versions of song form (AABA) or of simple strophic (verse – chorus or verse with refrain) forms" (Holm-Hudson 2008: 60). At 02:31 there is an interlude (B), as the band becomes quiet and Gabriel's vocals sing softly, before going back (03:13) into the main theme (A). Lyrically, we are introduced to the setting of New York (00:52) and the character and narrator Rael (03:58). Currie (1998) compares "the image of Rael "wiping his gun" (03:17) and "forgetting what he did" (03:19) "not to subway vandalism but an act of sexual violence." The mentioned lamb (00:40) ""isn't a symbol" for Christ, according to Gabriel; rather, it is merely "a catalyst for peculiarities that take place"" (Bell, 1975, p. 14 in Holm-Hudson 2008: 65). At the end of the song (04:20), "we hear the first of several references to songs of the 1960s in *The Lamb*, here a musical and lyrical quote from the 1963 Drifters hit "On Broadway"" (Holm-Hudson 2008: 65). This is the first of many songs on the album with a relative short length of 4 minutes 52 seconds. But there are also their usual trademarks on the album.

The following song, 'Fly on a windshield' "is an excellent example of how, in Tony Banks's words, "at times things were little more than improvisation on an idea" (Fielder, 1984, p. 91)" and it stands out for "the stylistic imprint of Steve Hackett", when it "begins with a delicate recitative-like passage with quiet guitar strumming accompaniment", followed by "a electric guitar solo over a heavy drum beat [...] and loud bass pedals" (Holm-Hudson 2008: 66).

In the song 'In the Cage', "there is evidently a play on various Biblical symbols" (Holm-Hudson 2008: 70), something known from songs like 'Supper's Ready'. The song 'Back in N.Y.C.' "was quite unlike anything else Genesis had recorded before" as it represents a mix of old trademarks and new ideas. It has a ""pedal point groove" over an asymmetrical meter, something that had been done before (for example in the "Apocalypse in 9/8" section of "Supper's Ready")" but "the lyrics, however, were a harsh jolt of reality. If Genesis could earlier be accused of having fey or twee lyrics, there was nothing fey about lines such as "I'm not full of shit", which Gabriel spat out with all the venom of a proto-punk-rocker" (Holm-

Hudson 2008: 75). The song also "prefigures the more stripped-down musical direction of Gabriel's first two solo albums" (Holm-Hudson 2008: 75) and together with the title track he "sometimes used the song as an encore on his first two tours" (Holm-Hudson 2008: 76).

They also tried to have another single hit: The song "The Carpet Crawlers" (also titled on some recordings as "Carpet Crawlers" or "The Carpet Crawl") is "along with the title track, the most beloved song on *The Lamb*" and "was chosen to be the second single from the album", and "it was a minor hit in the UK" (Holm-Hudson 2008: 79), not reaching the same position as 'I Know What I Like' did. The song features some typical playing of Tony Banks, whose "repetitive cascading arpeggios would later be heard on "Ripples" from *A Trick of the Tail*, Genesis's first post-Gabriel release" (Holm-Hudson 2008: 79). The song has a special place in Genesis history, as "all five members of the "vintage" Genesis line-up re-united for a new version of the song, which was included on the compilation *Turn it On Again: The Hits*" in 1999. The new version "is particularly interesting in that Gabriel and Collins share lead vocals on the song, ultimately harmonizing toward the end" (Holm-Hudson 2008: 79). Phil (Collins 2007: 167), when he first heard the song, "had a bizarre feeling listening to it", because he "knew it was Pete singing when the track started but then it went to a verse and I couldn't tell whether it was me or Pete." Steve Hackett (2007: 167) agrees that "both he and Pete had such similar and sympathetic voices that when they were singing together it sounded like doubletracking, wonderful harmonies on tunes like 'The Chamber of 32 Doors' or 'I Know What I Like'." This led to the simple idea that Collins became the new singer after Gabriel had left.

On the album Tony Banks makes interesting use of the Hammond organ, one of the elements that created Genesis' 'pastoral' sound and "although Tony Banks uses the Hammond in a *rhythm*-instrument capacity on this album (on "In the Cage" for example [...]) he does not use it for its *sustaining* qualities, that role being given to the Mellotron instead (as in, for example, "Hairless Heart")." This change "is tied to the desire to get away from the "liturgical", "English" aspects of Genesis's style and more toward a "secular", "American" style" (Holm-Hudson 2008: 81).

In 'The Lamia', Gabriel makes use of cultural reference as much of the lyrics "imagery is derived from John Keats's 1819 poem "Lamia"" (Holm-Hudson 2008: 86 f.). Musically, the song's "descending harmonic progressions are also found in the verses of Genesis's other water-related epics, "Fountain of Salmacis" and "Ripples")" (Holm-Hudson 2008: 87). It is being played by Tony Banks' Mellotron. The instruments association

"with the water imagery is a further link with "Fountain of Salmacis""
(Holm-Hudson 2008: 88) from the album *Nursery Cryme.*

Onstage, Gabriel overused the visual aspects for the songs of this album. For 'The Lamia' "a tube of multi-colored fabric descended, maelstrom-like, over Gabriel, obscuring him from view" (Holm-Hudson 2008: 89). For 'The Colony of Slippermen' he was wearing an outfit, which was "covering Gabriel head to toe in grotesque latex bumps, had two testicles made of balloons that could be inflated and deflated by a roadie." The "suit's oversized head didn't allow Gabriel's vocals to be heard clearly, because the microphone was too far from his mouth" (Holm-Hudson 2008: 89). The band was nerved by this exaggeration and felt that the costumes and the performance had become the focus of the show to the disadvantage of the music. Tony Banks says that was the point "when we thought that the balance had gone the other way" (Russell 2004: 208).

Lyrically, the song "is about "people's attitudes towards sex, a theme that would recur through much of Gabriel's solo work." Another cultural reference is the opening stanza, which "parodies William Wordsworth's 1804 poem "Daffodils"" (Holm-Hudson 2008: 90). Musically, "its structure is perhaps the most stereotypically "progressive" of the songs on *The Lamb*, being that of a multi-part suite with subtitles for individual sections ("The Arrival", "A Visit to the Doktor", "Raven")" (Holm-Hudson 2008: 90). It has "Japanese influences [...] as strange stringed instruments twang and chirrup and temple blocks clip-clop" in the intro and consists Genesis' progressive features such as "unusual time signatures, beats that stray across the bar and constantly shifting moods" (Welch 2005: 41).

The last song on the album, 'It', is the last time we hear Peter Gabriel singing with Genesis on an album. The penultimate song 'In The Rapids' "ends with a dramatic upward swoop on synthesizer, leading directly into "*it.*", an up-tempo song, whose "closing line "It's only knock and knowall, but I like it" is a punning reference to the Rolling Stones' 1974 hit "It's Only Rock and Roll"" (Holm-Hudson 2008: 95).

With songs like 'The Musical Box' and 'Supper's Ready' the band had proved to be a classic progressive rock band. Many features that characterize the genre also appear in their music. After *Selling England by the pound* and *The Lamb Lies down on Broadway*, one might notice some changes. According to Hegarty & Halliwell (2011: 61) "these albums [...] marked a distinct movement away from the folk-rock pastoral of early Genesis." Many features still appear in their music, others have changed. So what does the list of typical elements in Genesis music look like for their first era?

- A mixture of loud passages, soft passages, and musical crescendos to add to the dynamics of the arrangements:
    1. Compare e.g. the passages 'Lover's Leap' (00:00 – 04:40) and 'Willow Farm' (13:34 – 16:18) from 'Supper's Ready'.
    2. At the same time, a song like 'I Know What I Like' does not include any mixture of loud and soft passages or any musical crescendos at all.
- Extended instrumental solos, electric and electronic instruments where each plays a vital role in translating the emotion of compositions which typically contain more than one mood (cf. the whole of 'Supper's Ready')
- Acoustic versus electric sections (cf. the acoustic beginning of 'The Musical Box' and 'Supper's Ready' and their following electric passages)
- Very "picturesque" lyrics:

Recurring topics are mythology (in 'The Musical Box'), nature (e.g. 'How Dare I Be So Beautiful?'), religious lyrics ('Supper's Ready' as "a Gabrielesque vision of the battle of Armageddon and the second coming of Christ") and a certain kind of "Englishness" (e.g. in 'Willow Farm'). On *The Lamb Lies down on Broadway* the "Englishness" is avoided in favour of an "American" surrounding. The lyrics are often storytelling ('The Musical Box') and there are also a lot of cultural references in the lyrics (e.g. 'Winston Churchill' in 'Willow Farm' or the citation of The Rolling Stones in 'It').

- Visual material:
    1. Elaborate surrealistic album covers (cf. the covers of Nursery Cryme, Foxtrot, Selling England by the Pound and The Lamb Lies Down on Broadway)
    2. Elaborate stage shows (the costumes of Gabriel, e.g. "the strange box mask" in 'Apocalypse in 9/8' and other costumes)
- Form:
    1. Up to 1973: Embellishment of traditional shapes (AABA, verse-chorus), less reliance on traditional shapes; unconventional forms (Luck even names 'Supper's Ready' as an example of this)
    2. From 1973 on: The structure of the songs changed and became more direct and traditional (cf. the song 'The Lamb Lies Down On Broadway')

- Complex arrangements usually featuring intricate keyboard and guitar playing: Take Banks' keyboard solo in 'Apocalypse in 9/8' and Hackett's guitar playing in 'The Musical Box' (from 09:10 – 09:26)
- Songs predominantly on the longish side, but structured, rarely improvised:
    1. Up to 1973: The performance of 'The Musical Box' runs at a length of 09:39, the one of 'Supper's ready' runs at a length of 26:07.
    2. From 1973 on: The length of the songs changed and became shorter overall ('The Lamb Lies Down On Broadway' runs at a length of 04:42, 'Back in N.Y.C' runs at a length of 05:45, 'The Carpet Crawlers' runs at a length of 05:15)
- The use of Mellotron (the intro to 'Watcher of the skies', the solo in 'Apocalypse in 9/8')
- Multi-movement compositions that may or may not return to a musical theme. In some cases the end section may bear little resemblance to the first part of the song (the end of 'The Musical Box' does not resemble its beginning at all; the end of 'Supper's Ready' takes up the first part 'Lover's Leap' and repeats it)
- Rhythm & meter: Syncopations, tricky rhythms; less reliance on 4/4 time signature (cf. the 'Apocalypse in 9/8'-section, which, as the name reveals it, is in 9/8)

Those (especially the real 'progressive') features are what most fans of the 'old Genesis' appreciate. A slight change can already be noticed from 1973 on, namely the shift from longer to shorter songs and the shift from complex to simpler structures. Some of them were to be criticized when the band had shrunk to a three-men-band, but we will have a closer look at that later.

The Lamb Lies Down On Broadway "received decidedly mixed reviews", among them the critique "that Genesis had simply overreached this time" (Holm-Hudson 2008: 97). They "roasted the *idea* of the album [...] and the public merely treated it with indifference" (Bowler & Dray 1992: 94). Nowadays, "the album remains beloved by fans" (Holm-Hudson 2008: 97). Collins (*Genesis interviewed on The Lamb Lies Down on Broadway*, 46:28 – 46:46) admits that it was not liked when it came out, but it is looked upon now in a hazy retrospective because it is "Gabriel's "swan song" with the group, after which – progressive rock wisdom has it – the band took a sharp artistic nosedive by pursuing commercial success" as Holm-Hudson (2008: 143) names it. Mike Rutherford finds the most direct words when saying that "it was a commercial failure. People talk about it now as a Genesis classic, but at the time, it died a death" (Fielder 1984: 92).

Nevertheless, by the time the album was released, "its subsequent failure in terms of sales and reviews was unsettling and frustrating" (Welch 2005: 35), especially for Peter Gabriel. As they were touring the ambitious album ("we [...] played the entire album live with only one or two old songs at the end" says Rutherford (2007:158)), Peter Gabriel "had already secretly decided to leave the group". The spectacular stage show also brought along some problems: The slides at the back of the stage "sometimes stuck"; on one night, "Peter's dummy [for one of the songs] was replaced by a naked roadie" (Bowler & Dray 1992: 101) and once, Collins remembers, when there had to be a small explosion for one song,

> "our production manager mixed too much bang, and not enough flash, so the whole thing exploded [...] and we had to stop playing in the middle of the song. The bloke poked his head round the curtain and said "Sorry!" I remember shouting at him: "You're fired!"" (Fielder 1984: 94)

Peter "Gabriel played his last gig with Genesis at St Etienne in France in May 1975", where "he was cheated of an emotional fanfare because St Etienne was meant to be the penultimate date of the tour, but after that appearance the final date was cancelled" (Bright 1988: 64). Banks remembers, that "at Pete's final gig, he played 'The Last Post' in the dressing room – on the oboe" (Fielder 1984: 95). And so, Gabriel' time with Genesis was over. When it was announced publicly, "his fans were greatly shocked and many doubted if Genesis could survive without him" (Welch 2005: 35). They did and so did he. Tony Banks calls it "the end of an era" (Waller 1985: 40). After his departure, "Gabriel launched a highly successful solo career and with Phil Collins taking over as lead singer, Genesis would prosper for another 20 years" (Welch 2005: 36).

3.2.5   That Voice Again: Peter Gabriel's solo career

> "A lot of my new stuff is very emotional. Genesis wasn't the platform for personal songs, you couldn't have a good dose of self-pity. [...] I'll probably record an album soon, but there won't be any heavy sell solo career and I'm not going on the road yet because that would defeat a lot of the object I left the band for" Peter Gabriel in 1975 (in Bright 1988: 12)

Peter Gabriel became much more famous as a solo artist than in Genesis. However, when he was doing his first solo songs, his fellow musicians were "Anthony Phillips on piano, Mike Rutherford on bass, and Phil Collins on drums" (Thompson 2005: 146). His first hit was 'Solsbury Hill' from his first solo album, being called by Chris Welch (cf. 2005: 98) a quality pop song, which reached "number 13 in the UK chart in April, 1977" and was "the highest-charting 45 yet from the Genesis camp" (Thompson 2005: 148).

He carried on some of his trademarks from Genesis times throughout his career. 'Solsbury Hill' for example is in the strange metre of 7/4 (cf. Bright 1988: 82). The video (https://www.youtube.com/watch?v=_OO2PuGz-H8) shows some very Gabrielesque pictures of British landscape (00:18) and British behaviours (making of tea, 01:49) and some characters with strange costumes (03:35).

Gabriel still kept contact to the Genesis camp and he also helped shape Genesis' "pop" future in a little way: On his third album, Phil Collins played the drums and together with engineer Hugh Padgham they created a new "drum sound", which would also be used on Collins' "own solo album *Face Value*" (Welch 2005: 99) as well as on the next Genesis albums. Gabriel did not want any "cymbals and hi-hats" (Bright 1988: 99) on the album, so Collins started "fooling around in the studio on his kit", with the "extraordinary effect created by a new device called a gate compressor unit. [...] Peter was so delighted by the effect he wrote a song called 'Intruder', built around the new sound" (Welch 2005: 99). The album "established Peter as a major solo artist" (Welch 2005: 100).

A hit from *Peter Gabriel III* was 'Games without Frontiers', "Peter's first Top Ten single hit as a solo artist." Another important song from his third album is 'Biko', "a song about a South African political activist, who died in 1977" (Welch 2005: 100). It became "an anthem for the struggle across the world" and "put him into the political arena" (Bowler & Dray 1992: 235). The song became famous in 1987, when it was released for a film about Stephen Biko. Scenes from the movie are included in the video (cf. https://www.youtube.com/watch?v=MgM-1r0X5Zc). It is another concession to his love for film and visual effects. In an interview with Terry Wogan from 1987 (*Peter Gabriel – Wogan 1987*, 04:11), he says that music is "the first universal language all around the world" and he uses it as a possibility "to give out information" on subjects like the death of Stephen Biko. At the celebration of "Nelson Mandela's 70th birthday", Gabriel united "with Simple Minds for a deeply impassioned "Biko."" (Thompson 2005: 249).

Gabriel, by now being a famous solo artist as well as a political active celebrity, was being famous for his experiments with sounds, synthesizers, strange rhythms and noises. What had started on 'Intruder' was even more present on his next album. In the making of his fourth album (*Peter Gabriel on The South Bank Show 1983, Making of Securtiy*), one can see his ways of working: jamming with African drummers (07:50) in search of new rhythms, using a Fairlight CMI Synthesizer (16:07), which can sample every sound, smashing TV screens or blowing through pipes on a junkyard (17:00, 17:22).

Holmes (1985: 168) describes "the use of natural sounds and noise as a part of the music or as atmospheric material" and of course, "The Beatles were responsible for making this popular (note the use of crowd sounds and barnyard animals on *Sgt. Pepper's Lonely Hearts Club Band* in 1967)" and he writes three years after the release of *Peter Gabriel IV* that "countless groups used sound effects during the 1960s and 1970s and continue to do so today." He even thinks (in 1985: 156) that "the very heart and soul of rock music is a devotion to an experimentation with sound." Through that Gabriel moved away from Progressive Rock to world music, a genre he would define very much (cf. Thompson 2005: 195). His "research into different musical cultures" made him create "the WOMAD Festival in July 1982" (Bright 1988: 156), where he played together with musicians from all over the world. The festival "was financial disaster" and Gabriel received "horrible phone calls and death threats from people I owned money to". So, his old band Genesis offered their help and they performed, for one last time, one concert together "to pay off the debts" (Gabriel 2007: 246). They started with 'Back in N.Y.C', but also "the set included some post-Gabriel material including 'Turn It On Again', where Gabriel and Collins embraced each other while passing on stage as Collins went to the front to sing while Gabriel took over the drums." The surprise was perfect when the band, which "included newer Genesis recruits Chester Thompson on drums and Daryl Stuermer on bass", was completed by "Steve Hackett for 'I Know What I Like (In Your Wardrobe)' [and] 'The Knife'" (Bright 1988: 149).

Peter Gabriel continued to appear in strange outfits and make-up onstage (cf. the cover of *Peter Gabriel plays live album*) and his album covers were still very elaborate and surreal (cf. the cover of the single *No Self Control.*) His interests in visuals and performance reached their peak, when he wrote the soundtrack to the movie *Birdy*, that, according to Thompson (2005: 230) "also marked the end of Gabriel's most overtly experimental music phase" and that lead to "times when even the most patient fan began to despair of ever hearing a "new" Peter Gabriel album."

His biggest success was the album *So* from 1986 with the hit 'Sledgehammer', described by Welch (2005: 102) as "one of Peter's most exultant performances." The song is accompanied by its famous videos, which "was voted Best Video" in 1987 and showed his love for visual approaches. His stage costumes had developed into animated and spectacular music videos. The song itself "went to number one in the States for a week in July 1986 and sold a million copies worldwide" (Welch 2005: 103). On the great tour that followed the *So* album and featured his long-time fellow musicians "Tony Levin and David Rhodes" on bass and guitar and new top-players "Manu Katche" on drums and "David Sancious on keyboards" (Bright 1988: 215), Gabriel "discarded [...] face make-up" (Bright 1988: 216) and ended his onstage-costume-era. After this tour he fulfilled his dream of a 'Willow Farm' in a different sense: He took "much of his earnings from the album into the construction of a new state of the art studio [...], called Real World", which "is in rural area, open to natural light and so a far healthier and more inspirational setting in which artists can work." He created this place also for world-musicians "such as Nusrat Fateh Ali Khan", who can record "there at a very low cost" (Bowler & Dray 1992: 236).

Peter Gabriel had become a pop star in his own sense, avoiding long songs and creating hits like 'Digging in the dirt' from 1992, with its "symbolic obscurity" that forms Gabriel's lyric and that need an "accompanying video". The whole album *Us* was full of "illustrations, contributed by ten artists from around the world, that accompanied each of the song titles in the CD booklets" (Thompson 2005: 250). The album was "another solid chart success - #2 in the U.K. and U.S." (Platts 2007: 142).

Lyrically, he dealt with love (in 'Modern Love'), religious topics ('Blood Of Eden') and he continued to tell stories (in 'Moribund the Burgermeister').

It took ten years for Gabriel to release a new album, *Up*, it's highlight is "the orchestrated 'Signal To Noise' [...] with Nusrat Fateh Ali Khan, [...] about the need for sense of morality and compassion" (Welch 2005: 106). Peter described that he had found his own musical identity on songs like this one (http://www.youtube.com/watch?v=xJoSNZxLdbU), with its "string arrangements which I might have not had the confidence to try in the earlier years of my solo career" (Gabriel 2007: 163). Peter Gabriel, one of the biggest pop stars of our times, but still experimenting with music and sounds, had found his musical revelation in his solo career.

4. The development of the rock band Genesis Part II: The Phil Collins era

4.1 Dance on a Volcano: 1975-1977

The short period as a quartet is a difficult period for a lot of fans. For some, the 'classic' Genesis stopped when Peter Gabriel left them, for others the progressive rock era was over, when Steve Hackett left. Still, most fans agree that the two albums they did as a quartet – *A Trick Of The Tail* (1976) and *Wind And Wuthering* (1977) were still the band's classic "high-progressive style" (Holm-Hudson 2008: 148). As for the singer, the band "couldn't find anyone to do it, so it became logical for Phil to do it", remembers Tony Banks (Bowler & Dray 1992: 117). Another advantage was that his voice was similar to Peter Gabriel's. Funnily enough, Phil Collins first suggested that they should "carry on as a four-piece without any singing" (Collins 2007: 159). On their first tour without Peter Gabriel they even played for example the song 'Fly on a windshield' from *The Lamb Lies Down On Broadway* in "an instrumental version" (Holm-Hudson 2008: 66).

A little frustrated by "the fact that that people thought [and some still think] Peter had written everything" they decided to bring in individual songs and "credit each song to whoever wrote it" (Banks 2007: 167). This and the fact that the trio Banks, Collins, Rutherford were improvising again and created major parts of songs like "'Squonk' and 'Dance On A Volcano'" (Rutherford 2007: 168) frustrated Steve Hackett, who "was becoming increasingly unhappy that the band wasn't making enough use of his writing" (Welch 2005: 46). Also, "as Phil was still very much a fledging writer" (Bowler & Dray 1992: 112), Tony and Mike were the main songwriters for the following three albums. All these factors lead to Steve Hackett's departure in 1977.

As for the music, Genesis had not changed at all. Classic examples are the songs "Dance on a Volcano" and "Los Endos", the first and last song of *A Trick of the Tail*. The songs were segued together live as can be seen here in a live version from 1980: http://www.youtube.com/watch?v=hW66dxbgXS4. The guitar is played by Steve Hackett's live replacement Daryl Stuermer, the drums by Chester Thompson, who has played live for the band since 1977, as Phil had to focus on being the front man. Their drum-duets (as the one that combines the two songs, 04:30-05:37) would become legendary at the band's concerts. Phil Collins proofs that he is a typical progressive rock drummer, as he "variously elongated and shortened drum solos or embedded them in songs and medleys" (Hegarty & Halliwell 2011:

130) which stands in contrast to drum-solos in other genres like hard rock or heavy metal. The merging of the two songs on the other hand caused that the beginning of the studio version of 'Los Endos', "a few bars of desultory guitar" (Welch 2005: 45) were left out.

Welch (2005: 43) says that "while the old Genesis had begun to sound lost and in danger of repeating themselves", with songs like these they "make a huge leap forward" and Phil's voice sounds "powerful". 'Los Endos' is a typical Genesis-instrumental, where "themes interweave and tempos change" (Welch 2005: 45). The song reprises themes from 'Dance on a Volcano' and the song 'Squonk', which is "a big, fat rocker" (Welch 2005: 44) and lyrically a "return to myths and legends" (Bowler & Dray 1992: 120). Tony Banks thinks that 'Los Endos' is "the most adventurous track on the album" (Fielder 1984: 97).

The other songs on the albums carry on Genesis' trademarks from their last albums. The song 'Entangled' is "a pretty ballad by Steve Hackett and Tony Banks with 12-string guitars", drifting "into a hauntingly melodic climax with resounding chords, before the soporific guitars gently fade away" (Welch 2005: 44), dealing with "the perils that you might encounter on a psychiatrist's couch" (Hackett in Platts 2007: 84). The storytelling and the different characters also appear in the songs. On the title track 'A Trick of the Tail' "Phil sings with sparkling clarity and masterful narrative skill" (Welch 2005: 45) and on "Robbery, Assault & Battery" he acts "out this tale of a murderous safe cracker" (Welch 2005: 44). This, together with the title track and 'Ripples' was "the first ever Genesis promo video" (Welch 2005: 44). The Banks/Rutherford collaboration 'Ripples' features according to Welch (2005: 45) an "Elizabethan style folk melody" and has "one of the group's loveliest instrumental passages, built on the interplay between Banks' grand piano and the sensual backwards-guitar sound [from] Hackett" (Platts 2007: 84). Banks is playing his "repetitive cascading arpeggios" (Holm-Hudson 2008: 79), which he already used in e.g. 'Carpet Crawlers' and 'The Lamia'. Holm-Hudson (2008: 123 f.) notices that

> "water is a recurrent image in Genesis's music, both during and after the Gabriel years; notable examples include "Stagnation", "The Fountain of Salmacis", the "How Dare I Be So Beautiful?" section of "Supper's Ready", "Firth of Fifth", "Ripples", and "One for the Vine" among others."

"The epic *One For the Vine*", written by Tony Banks alone, is one of the standout-tracks on *Wind and Wuthering*, a song that "suggests that Genesis were out to recapture the story telling spirit of yore and it's a highly successful strategy" (Welch 2005: 47). The song's lyrics are "a complex tale of an ordinary man put forward as a Christ-like figure and forced to lead a people convinced of his invincibility into battle, a situation from which he has just fled" (Bowler & Dray 1992: 130). They add, that "the lyric is imaginative and intriguing" and "the music springs from a melting pot that bubbles with dynamic invention." Another highlight on the album is Steve Hackett's 'Blood on the rooftops', "which opened with a beautifully executed acoustic guitar piece" (Bowler & Dray 1992: 131), the lyrics full of "images from various TV shows and movies" and dealing with "the paradoxes and banalities of comfortable English life" (Welch 2005: 48). The most famous song of *Wind and Wuthering* is Banks' ballad 'Afterglow', called by Chris Welch (2005: 85) the "highlight of the album". It is "a concise love song" and it is "a sensitive, emotional and ultimately powerful song as anything among their previous works, yet it lasts little more than four minutes rather than the ten or fifteen minutes of past 'epics', losing none of its impact as a result" (Bowler & Dray 1992: 130). Banks says that while 'One for the Vine' "had taken over a year to develop [...], 'Afterglow' was written pretty much in the time it took to play it – it was a spontaneous piece, something I hadn't really done before" (Fielder 1984: 99). "Beginning in 1980", the song was to become the end of a medley in live performances, which included bits and pieces from Gabriel-era-songs and ended "with a complete performance of "Afterglow"" (Holm-Hudson 2008: 71 f.). The counterpart to Banks' 'Afterglow' is 'Your Own Special Way', "an outstanding pop song from Mike Rutherford" (Welch 2005: 47). It "was released as a single, reaching number forty-three" (Bowler & Dray 1992: 131). The combination Rutherford/love-lyric would become more successful on the next album, but no one knew at that point. In an interview from 1976 (*Tony Banks & Phil Collins Interview December 24, 1976*), Banks explains that on this album "it's the first time we've done love songs since *From Genesis to Revelation*" (34:35) and Collins adds that the band "can do exactly what we want [...] and we're just as happy or as proud, if you like, of something like '[Your Own] Special Way' as of [...] something like 'Supper's Ready' or 'A Trick Of The Tail'." (34:53)

A Trick of the Tail and *Wind and Wuthering* are albums that fulfil all the requirements for typical Genesis albums. If one looks at the list, one can see that there are:

- A mixture of loud passages soft passages and musical crescendos to add to the dynamics of the arrangements

In the video for 'Dance on a Volcano/Los Endos': the passages from 08:22 – 10:39 for loud and soft passages and 02:07 for a musical crescendo.

- Extended instrumental solos, electric and electronic instruments where each plays a vital role in translating the emotion of compositions which typically contain more than one mood (cf. 'Dance on a Volcano/Los Endos')
- Acoustic versus electric sections:

The Steve Hackett songs 'Entangled' and 'Blood on the rooftops' carry on the acoustic side of the band as it is played "with 12-string guitars" (Welch 2005: 44)

- Very "picturesque" lyrics:

They stay true to their recurring topics like mythology (in 'Squonk'), nature (in 'Ripples'), religion (in 'One for the Vine') and the "Englishness" (in 'Blood on the rooftops') and some psychological aspects in 'Entangled'; a more or less new subject is love (in 'Afterglow'), a subject that would become more important in the future. The storytelling is still there (as in 'Squonk' or 'One for the vine').

- Visual material:
  1. Elaborate surrealistic album covers (cf. the covers of both albums)
  2. Elaborate stage shows (cf. the already mentioned live version of 'Supper's Ready' from 1976)
- Form: Since 'I Know What I Like' the band began to toy around with simple, straight song formats. Complex structure (cf. 'One For The Vine') can be found here as well as a more simple structure (cf. 'Blood on the rooftops', 'Afterglow')
- complex arrangements usually featuring intricate keyboard (cf. 07:30 in the video) and guitar playing (cf. 10:04 in the video)
- Songs with different lengths, but structured, rarely improvised:

The suite 'Dance on a Volcano/Los Endos' runs at a length of 11:30, 'Afterglow' runs at a length of about 4 minutes.

- The use of Mellotron (in 'Entangled', cf. Thompson 1999-2004)
- Multi-movement compositions that may or may not return to a musical theme (cf. 00:00 – 00:15 with 08:22 – 08:44 in the video).
- Rhythm & meter: Syncopations, tricky rhythms; less reliance on 4/4 time signature (cf. the middle part of 'Dance On A Volcano' from 02:07 onwards, which is according to Banks (2007: 173) "played in 7")

The album *A Trick of the tail* received positive reviews throughout. It was called "a solid golden success" by Barbara Charone of *Sounds* (cf. Platts 2007: 86) and the *Rolling Stone* noticed, that "although the familiar themes are always apparent, A TRICK OF THE TAIL is much more straightforward, possibly because it's more a joint effort than the Gabriel-dominated albums" (Platts 2007: 86). The fans greeted the new "old" line-up of the band enthusiastically. Again no singles became hits, but the album "went to number three in the UK and reached 31 in the US *Billboard* chart", which was according to Banks "our biggest record and the first one to make any kind of sense in America" (Welch 2005: 43).

The process went on with *Wind and Wuthering*. It reached "#7 in Britain, while in America it peaked at #26" (Platts 2007: 92). Still, "reviews of *Wind and Wuthering*, where they would once have applauded Genesis's ability to maintain its proven course, now condemned its refusal to move with the times" (Thompson 2005: 141). This sudden change is due to the fact that "Britain's London-based music press had been championing a new musical movement, punk rock", a movement which stands for "a ferocious dislike of rock's monumental past" (Thompson 2005: 140). Genesis, "the heroes of '76, became the unwitting lepers of '77" (Bowler & Dray 1992: 128).

Next, they released one live album, *Seconds Out* as a foursome and Chester Thompson as live drummer, which included the latest Collins-sung versions from different songs: 'The Lamb Lies Down On Broadway' ("one of the more memorable themes and works well taken out of context", according to Welch 2005: 85) was combined with 'The Musical Box'; 'Dance On A Volcano', where "Phil sings a haunting refrain" was already combined with 'Los Endos', so that "the first and last tracks from *A Trick Of The Tail* are merged into one spirited show stopper" (Welch 2005: 86) and 'Firth Of Fifth' can be heard for the first time with two drummers, playing "clipped and restless", but for the last time with "Steve Hackett's guitar" (Welch 2005: 84). After this album, Phil Collins said, that "all Genesis needs now is a hit single. […] That really helps; otherwise you just remain a big cult" ("All we need's a hit", *Melody Maker*, April 2, 1977 in Platts 2007: 94). Steve Hackett left the band after the album and the hit was about to come – two factors which led to the split-up fan base.

4.1.1   Icarus Ascending: Steve Hackett's solo career

Steve Hackett made his first solo album between Peter Gabriel's departure from Genesis and their first album without him, *A Trick of the Tail*. He named the album *Voyage of the Acolyte*, which was "the first solo LP by a Genesis member" (Platts 2007: 78). On the one hand he was happy to create an album completely on his own, on the other hand his frustration grew as he had not that much material for the two forthcoming Genesis albums and the bits he had were not used most of the time. On the album there are nonetheless "Phil Collins on drums and Mike Rutherford on bass and 12 string guitar" (Welch 2005: 117) and the "wildly bizarre" (Bowler & Dray 1992: 238) instrumental song 'Ace Of Wands' (cf. http://www.youtube.com/watch?v=EGu0JhYjRmo) sounds just like Genesis on their albums at that time, consisting of changing moods (cf. 00:27 onwards and 00:48), loud (03:27) and soft (00:59) passages.

Besides from working with other Genesis-related musicians (e.g. "Bill Bruford, Chester Thompson and Paul Carrack [lead singer from Mike and the Mechanics]", Platts 2007: 141), Hackett carried on some of the Genesis features throughout his career. He kept continuing, perhaps more than the others in their solo work, the 'progressive rock' features. In his songs he was very often telling stories like 'Carry on Up the Vicarage' with its "touch of surrealism" and used mythological themes, for example on the song 'Narnia', which is based on "C.S. Lewis' children book (and Biblical allegory) *The Lion The Witch & The Wardrobe*" (Welch 2005: 117). He also wrote about love, for example in 'Can't Let Go'. Musically he carried on the acoustic guitar, "a love affair fully exposed on 'Bay Of Kings'" (Bowler & Dray 1992: 238) from 1983, an album solely played on acoustic guitar. His album covers were carrying on the picturesque artwork of Genesis, e.g. on *Please Don't Touch* or *Till we have faces*, which is created on the basis of the Genesis song 'Silent Sorrow In Empty Boats' from the album *The Lamb Lies Down On Broadway*. Similar to the "Genesis Archives" from the late 1990s, compiling "rarities and unreleased tracks" and "live tracks" (Platts 2007: 148), Hackett released "the four-CD LIVE ARCHIVE [...] featuring material from the '70s, '80s and '90s" (Platts 2007: 153) in 2001.

Hackett also tried to have some hits, releasing singles such as 'Clocks' in 1979 (cf. Bowler Dray 92: 239), but failed to gain success. His albums, however, sold quite well, ranging between position #9 and #70 in the charts (cf. Bowler & Dray 278 f.). One of his singles was the song 'Every Day' from 1980 (http://www.youtube.com/watch?v=SQaGCNGgfe4), which has a length of 6:15 and represents his style very well: The song consists of a unusual structure: Intro (00:00 – 00:29), verse (00:29 – 00:47), intro melody (00:47 – 01:01), verse (01:01 – 01:20), chorus (01:20 – 01:34), a quiet instrumental interlude (01:34 – 01:48), chorus (01:48 – 02:02), verse (02:02 – 02:20), intro melody (02:20 – 02:55), the interlude melody with full band (02:55 – 06:15), upon which he plays an extended guitar-solo. Over the years, Hackett played with a "range of influences from blues, classical and folk to jazz, rock and New Age music" (Welch 2005: 118).

If one compares the song 'Every Day' with 'Nomads' from 2009 (http://www.youtube.com/watch?v=K5XH4Vt-xHY) one can hear that Hackett had his own style, but never repeated himself and tried out different genres: The structure is quite identical, the song starts with his beloved acoustic guitar (00:00 – 00:39), before going over into a Latin-style acoustic number, over which he sings of a life as nomad. It runs until 02:29, a short break, then the piece becomes quicker and hands clap to the acoustic guitar solo. At 03:08 real drums set in and the solo is continued by an electric guitar.

The album, on which the song is featured, has another old Genesis guitarist as a guest musician: Anthony Phillips (cf. Genesis News Com). The two of them, although never having played in the band together, seem to complement each other, as both of them carried on the 'progressive side' of Genesis in their respective careers. Hackett still releases albums and tours extensively all over the world.

4.2   Like It or Not: 1977 - 1997

> "I remember, we were once described [...] as a folk/blues/jazz/ rock/mystical group" (Mike Rutherford in 'Three Dates with Genesis', 00:24)

After the departure of Steve Hackett the band "regrouped to make their next album" (Bowler & Dray 1992: 142). They called it ...*and then there were three*... "in a light acknowledgement of their reduced membership" and instead of searching for a new guitarist, Mike Rutherford "handled all guitar and bass duties in the studio" (Platts 2007: 101).

Banks remembers that "most of the album was written by Mike and I individually" (Welch 2005: 51), an example would be the single 'Many too many', "a finely wrought pop song" (Welch 2005: 53) written by Banks. But the most famous song from the album "was the only truly group-written song [...], the only one written from scratch in the rehearsal room." It "was the single 'Follow You Follow Me', their first to crack the UK top ten [...] and the song that introduced the group to a totally new audience" (Bowler & Dray 1992: 148). The song (cf. https://www.youtube.com/watch?v= h9zj11gf9Qk) was also "their first US Top 40 hit. It peaked at number 23 and stayed five weeks in the chart" (Welch 2005: 54). Welch thinks that it "remains one of the band's best liked songs from the mid-Seventies." Platts (2007: 102) adds that "Rutherford's lyric was perhaps the simplest set of words ever to grace a Genesis song", which, as he himself remembers, led to the effect that "the predominantly male audience was filled with girls. Wonderful!" (Bowler & Dray 1992: 149)

The song begins with Rutherford's guitar riff (00:01), on which the song was based, before the whole band sets in (00:12), Phil Collins playing "fun percussion effects, including bouncing bongos over a samba beat" (Welch 2005: 54). At 00:20 Collins starts to sing the verse, accompanied by Banks keyboards. At 01:03 "Phil sings the irresistible hook line", the chorus, before going back into the verse (01:24). Written by Mike Rutherford, "the lyric and message are simple enough", as Welch (2005: 54) names it. We can hear that as the chorus comes back (02:05). Tony Banks plays a keyboard solo (02:25) and the band goes back into the chorus (02:45) and repeat it until the end of the song (03:55). The keyboard solo is probably the shortest ever to appear in a Genesis-song up to that point and Welch thinks that "as the arrangements progresses, the instrumental parts come together in a neat and satisfying solution."

After their long, epic progressive rock songs, "having a hit with a three-minute pop song caused apoplexy among hardcore fans, leading to cries of 'sell out!'" (Bowler & Dray 1992: 148) Some critics were not particularly fond of the record either: "This contemptible opus is but the palest shadow of the group's earlier accomplishments. Not only is the damage irreversible, it's been highly endorsed: AND THEN THERE WERE THREE is Genesis' first U.S. gold record", says a review from the *Rolling Stone* magazine (Platts 2007: 102), one year after they have been blamed by the critics for being a progressive rock band in the punk age.

To be fair, one should not reduce the album to its hit single, just because it was the first one they had. The band was trying to have singles for years, as Banks says that "even things like "The Carpet Crawl" which I thought were good singles never were hits" (Bowler & Dray 1992: 150). He thinks that "'Follow You Follow Me' is close to 'I Know What I Like'" (Fielder 1984: 101), their first hit single that was loved by so many of their loyal fans. He also adds (in Banks 2007: 287) that 'Follow You Follow Me' was great for their future hits, because "even quite difficult songs like 'Turn It On Again' or 'Mama' [...] would get radio play." And live guitarist Daryl Stuermer remembers that "as soon as Genesis started having hit singles some old fans didn't like it. You'd see them turning up their noses when Phil announced 'Follow You Follow Me'. And I would think "Open up! Just because it's sold well, doesn't mean it's a bad song"" (Fielder 1984: 107).

The rest of the album is as "progressive" as Genesis ever were. Rutherford, who wrote the lyrics for 'Follow You Follow Me' also presented the composition 'Deep In The Motherlode', in which he shows his abilities as a lead guitarist, as "the guitars strike up a sprightly theme, set against the background of distant banjos" (Welch 2005: 52). Banks, who wrote the ballad 'Many Too Many' also provided 'The Lady Lies', which, with its "use of Hammond organ re-introduces a taste of old Genesis." It is a "seductive saga about a mythical character who is really a demon" (Welch 2005: 53). They were even thinking about putting three songs together as a little suite (cf. this fan-made video: http://www.youtube.com/watch?v=XKmk4LK3ov8), but in the end the section between 'Down and out' and 'Undertow' was left out and released as 'From the Undertow' on Tony Banks' first solo record (cf. Welch 2005: 119) a year later. Following the album, there was an ambitious tour, which introduced live guitarist Daryl Stuermer and which was reported about in the BBC-documentary *Three Dates with Genesis*. The new visual focus is on the "200 jumbo jet lights" (02:01), the band is described as "a sensible group" (06:37). It was also on this tour that Phil Collins' first marriage broke up – which led him to writing songs on his own. But this will become more important in the following chapters.

4.2.1   The song 'Turn it on again'

"The last GREAT Genesis album-oh how i miss those days when you could turn on the radio and hear 'watcher of the skies'.What happened? someone tell me" (youtube-user jltjr5's comment on the fan-made version of the 'Duke Suite').

NO STEVE HACKETT, NO PETER GABRIEL = NO GENESIS IDIOTA!!!! (youtube-user SPIRITWALKER IS SHIT's comment on the live version of 'Misunderstanding')

Get over it. The band has changed, Some would say negatively, i say positive (youtube-user Hingelable's comment on 'Turn It On Again Medley' from 1990)

Miss Hackett (youtube-user artois54's comment on the Concert from 1980)

'Turn It on Again' is an important song in Genesis' career. It was released "in March 1980" (Thompson 2005: 177) and was the "first UK single" (Bowler & Dray 1992: 164) from their album *Duke*. Tony Banks calls it "a classic Genesis song" (Welch 2005: 56) and music journalist Chris Welch (2005: 57) thinks it is "one of the best on the album." The single "reached #8 in the U.K. charts" (Platts 2007: 112 f.). The song's success allowed "them to appear on *Top of the Pops* in person for the first time" (Bowler & Dray 1992: 164) and promo videos were made for it as well as for 'Misunderstanding'. The album *Duke* sold well and "was the band's first number one UK album" (Welch 2005: 56).

In a live version from 1992 (cf. http://www.youtube.com/watch?v= kfCRv_4NuWk) the band plays the song "with their [...] touring band, augmented by long stay American friends Chester Thompson (drums) and Daryl Stuermer (guitar)" (Welch 2005: 87). Behind the stage there are big screens showing an animated road, as if someone is driving in a car along this desert road and listening to the "pulsating riff" (Thompson 2005: 177) played by Daryl Stuermer (00:01), which "Mike had [...] left over from *Smallcreep's Day* [his first solo album]" (Banks 2007: 216).

Genesis use one of their trademarks as Stuermer plays the bass pedals (00:17), creating "a static, often pulsating bass", over which "textures involving changing harmonies" would be played during the song. This was something that went back to "1972's "Watcher of the Skies"" (Holm-Hudson 2008: 60). "After counting in the tempo" (Welch 2005: 57), which is done by the audience (00:34), "a sharp keyboard motif" sets in, followed by "drums the size of Connecticut" at 00:49. The song consists "an unnaturally slippery time signature...most pop songs are in 4/4. [...] "Turn It On Again" lurched along in 13/8 – a rhythmic pattern that sounds more or less conventional until you try to tap your toes to it" (Thompson 2005: 177). Banks (2007: 247) says that "When you listen to the song you wouldn't think it contains anything odd, but when you start trying to play it you think, 'Where have I gone wrong?'"

Banks keyboards feature "a simulated brass section [...] introducing a funkier dimension à la Earth, Wind and Fire" (Bowler & Dray 1992: 164) to the song. In 1990, Genesis played the song at a music festival together with Phil Collins' touring band (cf. https://www.youtube.com/watch?v= TLVbogL3NLw). The horn section of his band was the horn section from "Earth, Wind and Fire", a fact Phil was very proud of: "They do EWF, the Jacksons and the Emotions but they don't do anything else. And here I was, young white boy, and they're playing with me. I was really chuffed!" (Bowler and Dray 1992: 168) The horns added a real "funky dimension" to the song, being a real brass section instead of the simulated one from the keyboards. Bowler & Dray (1992: 164) presume that the simulated horn section "indicated Phil's desire to further loosen Genesis' music." The fact that he used real horns in some of his songs and similar sounds were used in Genesis' music seems to proof that his influence in Genesis had become bigger. In this performance, the band stretches the song and includes some cover versions from other artists like "Everybody Needs Somebody To Love", "In The Midnight Hour" "Reach Out, I'll Be There" and "Pinball Wizard" (cf. Thompson 2005: 240). From 1983 onwards, "the band encored with a mutant version of 'Turn It On Again'" (Bowler & Dray 1992: 192) by turning it "into a medley that incorporated various rock and roll oldies plus the occasional contemporary cover" (Platts 2007: 130).

Continuing with the live performance from 1992, at 01:02 Collins starts to sing the lyrics "which Mike wrote" (Banks 2007: 219). The lyrics deal with someone watching TV, sitting at home because his girlfriend left him and starting to see the people on TV as his friends, which becomes clear as "Phil sings the memorable line "I can show you some of the people in my life..." and you wonder who they all are" (Welch 2005: 57) at 01:14. According to Banks (2007: 219) this was a topic that "was easy for people to relate to."

Welch (2005:87) explains that "Phil sings with great humour and skill, cleverly using echo to emphasise key phrases" at 01:39 and that "he shows complete mastery over the audience and song" as he lets them sing it (01:47). He (2005: 57-58) describes the part from 01:52 onwards as "doubled up Indian war dance backing beats" that "are irresistible." It seems true, as Collins performs some kind of dance at 01:57.

The song structure repeats itself from 02:00 on. Tony Banks said "that 'Turn It On Again' was originally a throwaway section used between two other bits" (Welch 2005: 56), but they thought that "this is much too good to be just a link" and "doubled it up, span out the chorus at the end and wrote a song on top to it" (Banks 2007: 216). The "pounding Indian war chant rhythm" (Welch 2005: 87) reappears in 03:01. At 03:10 the main theme starts again but instead of singing another verse, Phil sings the title of the song and at 03:20 "his cry of "Turn it on again!" becomes a jazz scat vocal as he tortures and toys with the words" (Welch 2005: 87). From 03:27 onwards Phil introduces the band. 'Turn It on Again' has at this point been the final song of the show for years and has always been the song in which Phil introduced the band to the audience. He introduces Daryl Stuermer (04:00), Chester Thompson (04:28) and Mike Rutherford (04:48), sings some lines from hits by his band Mike and the Mechanics (05:03), introduces Tony Banks (05:12), himself very shortly (05:33) and the whole band slowly becomes quiet (05:46). With a bang (05:48) they go back into the song, loud and heavy and Phil joins the rest of the band on the drums (06:24). They go into the ending part of the song (06:41) and end with a bang at 06:57.

The introduction of the band members and the ending of the song have always been the same, as can be seen in the version from 1990 with the

Phil Collins band, in which they played snippets of other famous songs. After its release, the song "became an integral part of Genesis shows henceforth", especially in later years, "as it invariably turned into an entertaining medley of favourite pop and soul hits" (Welch 2005: 57-58). Platts (2007: 130) thinks that "the reaction to the medley in some ways summed up the dilemma Genesis faced in trying to please the old and new fans" and quotes Phil Collins: "Some critics who like the show say, 'Why do they spoil it with that awful R&B?' Other people say 'We had to sit through two hours of boring music until we got to the R&B bit.' It's amazing." He remembers:

> "One night I just started singing a line from "Satisfaction" in it, a bit of "All Day And All Of The Night" [...] Everybody in the band was laughing, so then I got the John Belushi hat and shades and did the odd line from different songs and bit by bit people joined me and we took it to its conclusion with a medley!" (Bowler & Dray 1992: 192)

In tradition of Peter Gabriel, Phil slips into a role and dresses up for a song. In a live performance from 1984 (cf. http://www.youtube.com/watch?v=BfaOqnWcIoc), "songs featured in the medley included Everybody Needs Somebody to Love [05:38], Satisfaction [06:16], Twist and Shout [06:37], Pinball Wizard [08:47], All Day and All of the Night [07:07] and Karma Chameleon [07:44]" (Platts 2007: 130) as well as "'In The Midnight Hour' [09:22]", and "'Every Breath You Take' [08:27]" as "the medley grew nightly to the amazement of amusement of the fans" (Bowler & Dray 1992: 192).

The song was played on every tour since its release. They named a "Genesis hits package" (Thompson 2005: 275) after the song and when they announced their reunion tour in 2007 they appeared at the press conference "to the muted electric guitar opening of *Turn It On Again*" (Platts 2007: 155) and titled the tour "Turn It On Again – The Tour".

'Turn It On Again' is central to Genesis' history, for it "showed not only how good the band were getting at writing pop songs, but also how they could incorporate complex and challenging musical ideas into a song that seemed straightforward and simple" (Platts 2007: 111). Kevin Holm-Hudson (2008: 148) is of the opinion "that both ...*And Then There Were Three* and its successor, *Duke*, were decisive shifts away from the band's earlier high-progressive style." If you look at the song, its odd time signature and the other trademarks like the bass-line or the costumes on stage for the live-versions this may not seem appropriate. Another interesting fact is that on *Duke* "Collins, Banks and Rutherford originally intended to link all the group-written material (along with Banks' *Guide Vocal*) together as a 25-

minute suite that would take up one side of the LP" (Platts 2007: 111). In the end they decided not to do it,

> "since the group worried that the other side of the LP might sound weak by comparison, not to mention that fact that, in post-punk 1980, a 25-minute piece à la *Supper's Ready* would have strengthened the perception of Genesis as prog-rock dinosaurs" (Platts 2007: 111).

Nonetheless the suite was played live (cf. http://www.youtube.com/watch?v=YbNo14hMuU8 00:33:00 – 01:05:10) and there are Fan-made videos of the original songs linked together to one big song (cf. http://www.youtube.com/watch?v=Kd0jBZSeBjg). And even though "the songs were separated out [...] Mike Rutherford did hint at some form of conceptual string binding many of them together, namely a certain bewilderment at the nature of life in this strange new decade" (Thompson 2005: 178) and Tony Banks point out the song 'Duchess', which "combines all the best elements of modern Genesis" (Welch 2005: 57), by saying that "it's very simple but it has almost as much emotion as 'Supper's Ready'" (Bowler & Dray 1992: 164).

There are online discussions whether this suite or 'Supper's Ready' (cf. Turn It On Again – A Genesis Forum) are better liked. When played live, "the 'Duke Suite' was a monumental success, carrying all before it, becoming as integral a part of the set as hoary old favourites like 'Dancing With The Moonlit Knight' or 'The Carpet Crawl'" (Bowler & Dray 1992: 165 f.).

Phil gives an introduction before the "Duke Suite", telling the story of the main protagonist Albert (who can also be seen on the cover of the album). He makes fun with the audience and communicates with them. He makes a lot of jokes and refers to books and films of that time. That is also a trademark which the band carried on after Peter Gabriel left. So the criticism of a complete "shift-away" is not really true. After some member changes, the band even returned to writing together again instead of bringing in written material from each member. The fact that (almost) all the material of the suite was written by the trio Banks, Collins and Rutherford, just like the most important passages of 'Supper's Ready', "the closing section of *The Cinema Show*" (Platts 2007: 108) or of the album *The Lamb Lies Down On Broadway* "was the final confirmation that the magic of Genesis did indeed lie in the three of them working together as a unit" (Bowler & Dray 1992: 165 f.).

An important fact is that Tony and Mike had both released their first solo records prior to *Duke* and Phil had begun to write demos for his first solo album. So he became more of a songwriter himself and since they had all written songs individually for their solo records they could go back to the process of just rehearsing and improvising and create songs out of that instead of bringing in self-written material like they had done since Peter's departure (cf. Rutherford 2007: 218). They did of course bring in individual songs themselves. Phil's songs were 'Please don't ask' with "a very personal lyric" (Fielder 1984: 104) and 'Misunderstanding', which was one of the first songs for Genesis he had ever written all alone (cf. Platts 2007: 108). Funnily enough it was this song (cf. http://www.youtube.com/watch?v=OLH32F6Xvkw) that became "a Top Twenty hit in the US, peaking at number 14" (Welch 2005: 57) – a hint on Phil's solo success in the future. The song is called "a well rounded, satisfying soulful pop song" by Welch (2005: 57), who also thinks "that it is in direct contrast to the remnants of old Genesis." In his opinion "the band sound like they are enjoying it" (something you can see in the video as well). It starts with "a groovy beat" (00:01), "influenced by The Beach Boys" (Platts 2007: 110). At 00:20, Phil Collins starts singing "about a missed meeting and a wait in the rain with affecting simplicity" (Welch 2005: 57). At 01:00 "the band lock into a great swinging groove" (Welch 2005: 89) and at 01:28 they go back into the chorus, Phil sounding "hurt and injured" and "once again he shows you can't beat a simple, direct and uncomplicated lyric." The structure is fairly simple and repeats itself until 03:00, when the band becomes very laid back and gives Phil room to improvise with the lyrics, followed by an "abrupt, unexpected ending" at 03:46, which "is a treat" (Welch 2005: 89). The song is very different from their musical and lyrical epics. It represents Collins' style of writing, which is "very personal and direct" (Platts 2007: 108) and became an influence on the music of the band. Collins says: "I'm not afraid to say 'I love you' in a song – or even to make myself look a bit of a wally. People ask whether I get embarrassed revealing my private thoughts and emotions in a song and maybe looking a bit soft – but I don't" (Waller 1985: 56). The live version is taken from *Three Sides Live*, their first "concert film shot" (Thompson 2005: 190) later to be released for home video. It includes their hits and strongest live songs from that period, especially newer ones like the opener 'Behind The Lines', "a grand musical odyssey", where Phil "emerges from his beloved drum kit to hit centre stage", 'Abacab' or the last song, 'Turn It On Again.' The older songs were presented in one of the now established medley, which ended in "a beautiful treatment" of 'Afterglow'. This "splendid performance" (Welch 2005: 89) also presented the band's "new light show", the so-called "Vari-Lights, a computer-powered display that would soon become *de rigueur* among so many touring parties" (Thompson 2005: 190). Another different visual effect that replaced the costumes from the early days on the little stages.

The critique on *Duke* was very mixed. Chris Bohn of *Melody Maker* "played upon the recent publicity about the demand for tickets, and sported the headline, "Yes, half a million can be wrong."" Fan reactions to his review include the statements "he reduced almost a decade of instrumental and compositional wonder to a few unjustified paragraphs" on the one hand and "full marks to him for slagging off Mike Rutherford's and Tony Banks' nauseatingly narcissist rubbish" and "Congratulations to Phil Collins on almost saving the album" (cf. Platts 2007: 113) on the other one. The *Rolling Stone* was not that hard, admitting that since

> "THE LAMB LIES DOWN ON BROADWAY, Genesis have lapsed into a stylistic predictability that sorely misses Gabriel's perverse wit and the sensual near-Indian strains of Hackett's guitar. Yet the familiar, almost aesthetic sound of DUKE is comforting; a reassurance that Genesis aren't ready for an exodus yet" (Platts 2007: 113).

4.2.2 The song 'Abacab'

> "A lot of the die-hards will say that this was the begining of them diving off the cliff. But there was a couple fo really strong songs on Abacab. 'Sarah Jane' & 'Keep it Dark' my 2 favorites.Their sound sonically really leaped up on this album. The cover hwoeevr, sucks." (youtube-user stevedrums' comment on the live version of 'Abacab')

Phil's influence on songwriting as well as his success as a solo artist were a big contributor to their next album *Abacab,* which "to many marks both an artistic and commercial watershed in Genesis' evolution" (Bowler & Dray 1992: 154). It helped them to "build on their worldwide popularity while also showing a marked musical departure from their previous releases" (Bowler & Dray 1992: 154). It is the last album to feature solo-compositions (one song from each member) and it was the first to be recorded and produced in their new own studio, another factor that contributes to the musical evolution of the band. They bought the "Fisher Lane Farm in deepest Surrey" (Bowler & Dray 1992: 169) and hired a new producer, Hugh Padgham after working with their previous producer David Hentschel since *A Trick of the tail* (cf. Dodd 2007: 168). Padgham "had worked with Collins on FACE VALUE" (Platts 2007: 116) and with Peter Gabriel on his third solo album as well as with artists like XTC or The

Police (cf. Dodd 2007: 259). The band also hired "the Earth, Wind and Fire horn section", with which Phil had worked since his first solo album, for the song "No Reply At All" (cf. Thompson 2005: 187). They even made a joke about the punk movement by including a punk rock song on the album ('Whodunnit?', cf. Collins 2007: 234). The band, as Tony Banks said "tried to avoid our clichés" (Bowler & Dray 1992: 170), and Mike Rutherford explained that "the record sounds more like we do it in the rehearsal room" (Bowler & Dray 1992: 171). He adds that "we were becoming a caricature so we threw all that away and worked on the ones that were a little different." Or in other words: "We don't give a shit how people are going to react" (Rutherford in Fielder 1984: 106). Bowler & Dray also think that on the album that Phil Collins was "undeniably more confident than ever before and [was] having a greater input." Tony Banks (2007: 234) saw it as "an interesting exercise, and I think pretty successful too, particularly the track 'Abacab' itself and 'Keep It Dark', another favourite track of mine, both of which are very succinct tracks with a definite identity."

The chart success for the band went on, as "the title track 'Abacab' and 'Man On The Corner' were also hits in the UK and the US" (Welch 2005: 60). 'Man on the Corner' was Phil's solo song, nodding thematically in the direction of his later hit 'Another Day in Paradise'. Another single was the already mentioned "Keep It Dark" (cf. Bowler & Dray 1992: 176). The album itself "was the group's second U/K number one and their first US Top Ten platinum album" (Welch 2005: 60).

The album came out in September 1981, and "in August 1981, British fans got their first taste of the new Genesis with the release of the *Abacab* single" (Platts 2007: 118). The song exists in two different versions: The "necessarily brief hit-single version" and the album version, which was typical for Genesis as it was "stretched out across a dynamic seven minutes" (Thompson 2005: 189). The song "climbed to #9" (Platts 2007: 118) in England and "peaked at #26" in North America (Platts 2007: 120), which allowed them to appear at Top of the Pops again (cf. https://www.you tube.com/watch?v=5BSEbDEW8_k).

The track opens "with a burst of drums" (Bowler & Dray 1992: 174), followed by "a rocking keyboard riff" (Welch 2005: 61) at 00:05. From 00:20 onwards, the keyboard "contrasts with some grinding guitar from Mike", while "the drums hit a back beat" (Welch 2005: 61). As Phil starts singing (00:28) he "stabs out the phrases in staccato bursts" (Welch 2005: 61). Platts (2007: 118) describes it as "a stripped-down, driving number", which underlines Mike's opinion that the whole album has "got a lot of space"

(Bowler & Dray 1992: 171). Hugh Padgham, the producer, adds his part to it, as he "was more interested in rhythmic things" (Bowler & Dray 1992: 171 f.) than in the big, overwhelming keyboard-oriented sound from previous releases.

At 00:56 the chorus starts, Phil is "tough, concise, and shouting with confidence" (Welch 2005: 61), proving his satisfaction about his influence on the music. The word "Abacab", which is sung

> "came from the way it was written, as Mike explained: 'The song was made up of three bits, bit A, bit B and bit C, and that was the order they were in at one time. It's not right now, but it was just a nice word and it stuck when we came to write the lyrics!'" (Bowler & Dray 1992: 174)

Phil Collins gives yet another explanation: "A is Booker T and the MGs, […], B is the Rolling Stones and C is 'Friday On My Mind' by the Easybeats. It's very much a group song – there are bits from everyone on that" (Waller 1985: 82).

At 01:11 the verse comes again with "Mike's guitar riff […] echoed by a keyboard phrase from Tony" (Bowler & Dray 1992: 174). Thompson (2005: 189) calls the song "a punching, throbbing, behemoth of a number", which "packed a brutal electro enthusiasm that was absolutely in keeping with the harsher aspects of the so-called synthipop/New Romantic movement then holding Britain and, across the ocean, the fledging MTV in its thrall." Especially Tony Banks' keyboards really sound like he describes it, creating "squeaking, squealing, and burping" sounds.

At 01:41 the chorus starts again, followed by a middle passage (01:55), which reminds Bowler & Dray (1992: 174) of "an extended jam where they were very definitely casting a glance over their shoulders to *The Lamb Lies Down On Broadway*." The passage has some similarities to passages from the album, e.g. from *In the Colony of Slippermen*. At 02:31 the verse starts again, notable for one of their usual trademarks: "a static, often pulsating bass", as in "1972's "Watcher of the Skies" and "Turn it On Again"", over which they create "textures involving changing harmonies" (Holm-Hudson 2008: 60). At 03:08 the chorus comes again and then the intro is repeated (03:25) and the song fades out.

The studio-version of the song has a long instrumental passage at the end. When played live, they played the song full length, as can be seen and heard in a live version from 1984: https://www.youtube.com/watch?v=nE2 EV1gqIk4.

In the beginning, "the band zooms straight into the staccato rhythm that characterises the piece" (Welch 2005: 88). The song follows its usual structure until the end of the third chorus. From 04:17 on, the song does not fade out, but as Chris Welch (2005: 61) puts it: "Strange noises permeate the single note beat bashed out during an extended instrumental work." He (2005: 88) hears "a touch of *The Twilight Zone* from Tony Banks" and he also mentions the "the bass guitar" and its "single note pulse" throughout the song, which is "broken up by crashing cymbals" at 08:06. He (2005: 61) concludes that this passage is "extended instrumental work", which includes "jazz, rock, classical and funk music all compressed and distilled into a strange and highly potent blend" (Welch 2005: 88). This is progressive rock, as Hegarty & Halliwell (2011: 10 f.) proclaim it as a "highly experimental music [...] which linked together rock, jazz and folk scenes."

The bass is not the only similarity between this song and 'Watcher of the skies'. For both songs single-versions were produced, "*Watcher* also tagged on a fade-out refrain at the end" (Platts 2007: 55). However, in contrast to 'Abacab', "*Watcher of the Skies* [...] didn't chart" (Platts 2007: 57). So, the accusation of "just writing hits" and drifting away from their glorious, progressive past does not seem appropriate. They did the same thing with "Watcher of the skies" when Peter Gabriel was still singer. They use similar musical trademarks; the length of the song is typical. Also, "there has been speculation that the group intended to join several albums' tracks together in a suite, like the planned "Duke Suite" (Platts 2007: 118). A fan-made-video can be found here: https://www.youtube.com/watch?v=l--bZDQMrSI

Still, songs from the new album were "routinely booed when they played [...] live" (Thompson 2005: 188). And Bowler & Dray (1992: 176) say that "while 'Abacab' felt at home on stage, in general the new songs suffered the inevitable comparisons with 'Dance On A Volcano', 'Firth Of Fifth' or 'In The Cage'." At this time, fans wanted to hear the old songs instead of the new ones, but when they played the old songs, they were being criticized because of course they, and especially Collins, could not reproduce Gabriel's spirit (cf. the chapters about 'The Musical Box', 'Supper's Ready' and 'I Know What I Like'). The song itself was played on the following tours up until 1987.

Interestingly, the critics who had criticized *Duke* very badly, called *Abacab* "the most exiting and innovative music Genesis have made for years" and "deemed it "far more promising" than AND THEN THERE WERE THREE or DUKE" (Platts 2007: 119). In an article from the magazine *Sounds* ('Three Wise Men' by Cathi Wheatley, *Sounds*, 26 September 1981) it is said that "Post-Gabriel Genesis have progressed on every album since *A Trick Of The Tail* and *Abacab* is no exception" (in Bowler & Dray 1992: 176).

She adds that "the title track is probably one of the best things that Genesis have ever done – raunchy, lively stuff showing Collins at his most streetwise and all three at their most innovative" (Waller 1985: 85).

Tony Stratton Smith summarizes it very nicely: "Everywhere people were screaming betrayal, that Genesis had changed…and they were exactly the same people that were buying Pete [Gabriel]'s albums and celebrating the fact that every one was so different from the one before" (Thompson 2005: 188). *Abacab* was definitely influenced by the fact that "Phil suddenly became a big star during the making of the album" (Banks in Welch 2005: 60). The positive side was the album's chart success and as Phil Collins points out in an interview from 1982 (*Genesis – Three Sides Live – Interview (part 1)*): "There's really no threat at all to the group's existence by the fact that we all do solo albums. […] I think it's been very positive for the group" (04:06). The negative side of the success for the band was that "in the public's eye we were back to being a singer with a group, the very same perception we had experienced with Peter" (Banks 2007: 239).

4.2.3   The songs 'Home By The Sea/Second Home By The Sea'

Phil, you are awesome. (youtube-user Stuart Toyn's comment on the live-version of 'Mama')

its just genesis, not phil collins and genesis! (youtube-user Kamren Apelskog's comment on the live version of 'Mama')

Since the band had released *Abacab*, Phil Collins had become famous as a solo artist with his first two albums *Face Value* and *Hello, I Must Be Going*. So from their next album as a band, "the press expected a Genesis LP to be *Face Value* with louder keyboards" (Bowler & Dray 1992: 187). The group's answer was "the single *Mama*, released in Britain in August 1983" (Platts 2007: 128). The song had, according to Welch (2005: 64) a "unique style and sound" and Bowler & Dray (1992: 188) write that "in a chart filled with Culture Club, Wham, Spandau Ballett and similar pop stuff, it stood out a mile."

The song (cf. a live version from 1990: http://www.youtube.com/watch?v=uqv_ccG6yOo) "reached #4 in the UK charts" (Platts 2007: 128). It starts with "the drum machine" (00:00) and "its grinding beat [which] is joined by synthesised noises (00:29) that approximate the fluttering rotors of a probing helicopter" (Welch 2005: 65). Welch thinks that "the song smokes and reeks with atmosphere" and that Phil, as he starts singing (01:32) "emerges from a harsh, cruel soundscape to offer the plaintive cry of a lost soul wandering abroad in the city." Together with "his famous maniacal laugh and accompanying growls" (03:11) it makes the lyrics very picturesque and Welch interprets them as "a battle between good and evil, man versus the machine." Musically, "this hint of evil and despair is assuaged by Tony Banks' spiritual chords" (03:45). At 04:37 it is getting stronger, as the "heavy drum beat" sets in. Interestingly, the laugh in the song was "inspired by Grandmaster Flash's *The Message,* which Hugh Padgham had brought into the studio during the sessions" (Platts 2007: 128).

The single was backed with 'It's Gonna Get Better', a song that "started with an atmospheric Banks chord sequence – shades of *Watcher of the Skies* – under which a soulful bass line kicked in" (Platts 2007: 128). The new album, which consists the two songs, was "titled simply Genesis" (Platts 2007: 128) and Welch (2005: 64) sees the choice of the title as a hint for "an obvious pride and confidence in the project." He also calls it "one of the most impressive albums of the early Eighties."

Among the songs of the album, "tracks like 'Mama', 'Home By The Sea' and 'Silver Rainbow' could only be Genesis" (Bowler & Dray 1992: 190) and Thompson (2005: 212) thinks that they were "the most successful numbers" from the album, as they "retained the most readily identifiable elements of Genesis's past."

'Home by the Sea' was to "become a fan favourite and a staple of the group's live shows" (Platts 2007:128). A live version from 1984 can be found here: https://www.youtube.com/watch?v=8ibOkBudIHg. During live performances Phil Collins would tell a "ghost story" and together with the audience, try to reach the "other world". This made him able to "deflate the hugeness of the arena with some humour, mocking the traditional rock poses", something which he thinks is "very important [...] if you have dramatic songs" (Bowler & Dray 1992: 191). The end of his introduction can be seen on the video, before the song starts with a guitar riff (00:19). At 00:22 the whole bands set in and at 00:45 Phil stops singing the intro and goes into the verse. The song is "telling the story of a haunted house" (Bowler & Dray 1992: 190) and Welch (2005: 65) notices that the song is all "about images, memories, nostalgia and dreaming", its lyrics being written by Banks. At 01:05 they reach the first chorus, before going back into the verse (01:19). The chorus is repeated (01:40), this time longer than the first time (including the repeated call "Sit down!", 02:04), and it runs up until 02:26, where "a Japanese tinged melody prevails" as Welch (2005: 65) calls it, before it goes back "into its companion piece" (02:56). The whole structure is repeated (including an even longer chorus at 04:10) up until 05:34, where Phil joins the drums and the second part of the song begins. Bowler & Dray (1992: 190) see "the drums [...] more of a driving force than in the past, the playing tighter".

The following instrumental part 'Second Home By The Sea" is "a typical example of the group writing approach", as "Collins started playing a drum riff that appealed to Banks and Rutherford, and the trio jammed on it for several hours, refining it until the song took shape" (Platts 2007:128). Banks (2007: 263) remembers that "we listened back to it and clocked the parts we liked, learnt what it was we'd played and then repieced it back together", which "was another new way of working, and something we couldn't have done without the comfort of our own studio." This method can be seen in the video of the Making of the album (*The Making of the Mama Album {DVD Bonus Disc} – Genesis [Movie Box] (1984)*) from 27:36 onwards. 'Home by the Sea' "and its instrumental follow-up *Second Home by the Sea* allowed the band to stretch out in the classic Genesis fashion" (Platts 2007:128). In the Making of one can also see producer Hugh Padgham (for example at 02:07), who had a great influence on the sound of Peter Gabriel's, Phil Collins's and the band's albums of that time. Holmes (1985: 156 f.) points out that "even record producers become known for the styles they impart on record."

'Second Home by The Sea' is an "elongated instrumental section that had all the hallmarks of the early Genesis" (Bowler & Dray 1992: 190). Welch (2005: 65) compares the "furious instrumental section" with "violent storms [that] seem to batter the home by the sea." He also points out "the pristine clarity of the production, the fury of the drums and magical mixture of keyboard and guitar effects."

At 11:01, the instrumental part is over and Collins returns to the microphone (11:16) to sing one last chorus, while the band calms down after the heavy section. Thompson (2005: 212) sees the two-part song as "an almost-traditional epic, awash with dynamic instrumental passages" and Bowler & Dray (1992: 190) call it "an eleven-minute extravaganza in two sections" and "a treat for the traditionalists."

After *Genesis* the band took off into new heights. The next single from the album, 'That's all', described by Tony Banks (2007: 263) as "Beatle-ish", was "their first American Top Ten hit" (Welch 2005: 65). Another hit was 'Illegal Alien' with its "light hearted, semi-comic video" (Welch 2005: 66). The song was also full of sound effects, as trumpets, telephone sounds or car motors. The recording of these sounds can be seen in the video of the Making of from 12:05 onwards. The album itself was called by *Rolling Stone* "their safest album to date" (Platts 2007: 130). Waller (1985: 124) thinks that by this album, "the band had developed a unique style of blending together their own individual musical inputs to create a forever-shifting group sound." The concert in 1984 in Birmingham, of which the live versions are taken, was getting a royal touch, as "the presence of the Prince and Princess of Wales [...] added to the hubris of the "ordinary" fan" (Thompson 2005: 215). The new songs were well received live, especially 'Mama', where Phil would do the laugh over a green light, just like Peter Gabriel used to do it as Old Henry in performances from 'The Musical Box', 'Illegal Alien', where a choir of roadies joined the band (everyone in sunglasses) onstage and of course 'Home By The Sea' and 'Second Home By The Sea'. The concerts' release as "yet another live video, *The Mama Tour*" (Thompson 2005: 224) and its broadcast on the newly established music channel MTV helped to spread the band's success as well as so-called "Genesis MTV Video Weekends" (cf. *MTV Genesis/Friday Night Video Fights 1983 Promo*), where Genesis and Phil Collins videos and concerts were broadcasted. Their next two albums, *Invisible Touch* and *We Can't Dance* were to make them rock superstars. And MTV and the music videos had a great influence in that.

4.2.4   The albums Invisible Touch & We Can't Dance

i hate this song. bring me back real genesis (youtube-user desperation mixtape's comment on the live version of 'Invisible Touch')

im shocked to see the differences between invisible touch and suppers ready what great musicians they used to be :((youtube-user roger waters' comment on the official video of 'Invisible Touch')

One of the best examples of that Collins/Banks/Rutherford magic formula!!! (youtube user Leonardo Lotti's comment on the official video of 'Throwing It All Away')

The period from 1986-1993 "was the biggest we ever got", as Phil Collins (2007: 263) remembers. The gap between albums had become bigger since Phil had started his solo career. After the *Genesis* album Mike Rutherford had formed a new band, titled Mike and the Mechanics together with vocalists Paul Carrack and Paul Young (cf. Thompson 2005: 223), a band that became successful themselves. Tony Banks, having published solo-albums since 1979, did have no chart success. *Invisible Touch* was released three years after *Genesis* and was "a vibrant hit packed album" (Welch 2005: 67) including ""Tonight Tonight Tonight", "Land of Confusion", "In Too

Deep", "Throwing It All Away" and "Invisible Touch" itself" (Thompson 2005: 224). They had again recorded it with Hugh Padgham at the Farm (cf. Welch 2005: 67).

The song 'Invisible Touch' is often "regarded by the loyal progressive-rock aficionado as a betrayal" (Holm-Hudson 2008: 133), as it "represents Genesis at its most commercial." But the song was, just like all the songs on the album, "a product of group jamming" (Platts 2007: 133). In a live version from 1987 (cf. https://www.youtube.com/watch?v=cK3N2DC3Fds) the band plays the song at Wembley Stadium, which they sold out "four nights in a row" (Banks 2007: 287) and where they played incredible versions of well-known songs like 'Mama', 'That's All', 'Home By The Sea' (including it's meanwhile standard ghost-story introduction), one of the meanwhile established drum duets of Thompson and Collins going over into 'Los Endos' or the familiar 'Turn It On Again Medley' as well as from songs from the new album like 'Domino', 'Tonight Tonight Tonight', 'Throwing It All Away' with its call-and-response or 'Invisible Touch' itself (cf. Platts 2007: 134). Banks thinks that for him the four nights at Wembley were "the peak of our career." It was to become another live video release (cf. Bowler & Dray 1992: 207) and later on, in November 2003, the concert was released as *Live at Wembley Stadium* on DVD (cf. Platts 2007: 153).

'Invisible Touch' opens with a drum-machine (00:01), before the band sets in (00:23) with "Mike Rutherford's opening guitar statements that were the original inspiration for the piece" as Welch (2005: 68) informs us. The music is "pure pop" to him, but still "a joyous celebration of love, live and the mystery of human contact." At 01:06, "Collins' exultant cries of: "She seems to have an een-vis-ible touch, yeh-ah!"" (as Welch calls it) form the famous refrain. He also praises "the reassuring bass line" (cf. 01:20) and Tony Banks, who "flies off into keyboard heaven with a delirious solo" (02:04). The version runs for about five minutes.

But one should not judge the whole album from one song. 'Tonight Tonight Tonight' is according to Welch (2005: 68) their "most memorable pop ballad", with "a nagging electronic theme" and lyrics that "are alternately obscure and direct." The song "pulled together all the various strands of their career" (Bowler & Dray 1992: 202), its length "is about nine minutes" (Platts 2007: 134), including a middle section with "a series of suitably weird instrumental effects" (Welch 2005: 68). The song (the working title was 'Monkey/Zulu') "is an excellent indication of how Tony in particular will stretch the others" and "just as they were improvising the music, some of the lyrics were spontaneous too" (Bowler & Dray 1992: 202). 'Domino' is another 14-minute epic (cf. Thompson 2005: 224), "presented in two parts" (I. 'In the Glow of the Night', II. 'The Last Domino'), which are very different from each other, as "part One begins slow and pretty until an abrupt, stabbing explosion [and] the tempo doubles for Part Two" (Welch 2005: 69). The last song on the album is the instrumental 'The Brazilian', which is "the strangest and most demanding cut on the album, […] a re-affirmation of the band's faith in its musical past, […] full of spacey sounds like a sea monster, breathing heavily and stomping up the beach" (Welch 2005: 70).

The album was their most successful and granted by the critics. Songs like "'Invisible Touch', 'Land Of Confusion' and 'Tonight, Tonight, Tonight' would dominate international charts throughout 1986/87" (Welch 2005: 67). 'Invisible Touch' was also re-released as a live-version in 1992 (cf. Platts 2007: 165).

A factor that became very important at that time was the medium of the music video. Genesis had done some "promotional films" in their past, but in the 1980s "art video and music video arrived at the type of conjunction we know best: MTV" (Barbara London in Keazor & Wübbena 2010: 64). The music video is according to Keazor & Wübbena (2010: 7) "marking and shaping our every day culture; film, art, literature, advertisements – they all are clearly under the impact of the music video in their aesthetics, their technical procedures, visual worlds or narrative strategies." And Paolo Peverini (in Keazor & Wübbena 2010: 135) adds, that music videos "use expressive potentiality of different languages (visual, musical, verbal) in order to combine the commercial aims of the music business with original aesthetic experiments." Genesis made no exception as it came to music clips and they produced some of the finest and best-known music videos from the 1980s and 1990s. For almost every single since 'A Trick of the Tail' promotional videos had been produced. This song, together with 'Ripples', 'Follow You Follow Me', 'Turn It On Again' and 'Abacab' showed the band just playing the song, but as they went along a lot of videos were produced that had a story and were made up quite extraordinary. 'Misunderstanding' shows Banks and Rutherford playing their instruments on the back of a driving truck, while Collins drives in a car behind them and sings; 'Keep It Dark' sees them walking around city and landscape with mini-versions of their instruments; 'Illegal Alien' is a hilarious video, in which, "complete with Mexican accent, and fake moustaches Phil and the chaps emulate a hubbub of aliens attempting to enter the United States" (Welch 2005: 66); 'Mama' places them in a hot brothel and 'That's All' places them as homeless guys in an old factory building.

They made their most famous video for the song 'Land Of Confusion', which was next to 'Domino' the other anti-war song on the album. The lyrics were written by Mike Rutherford (cf. *Genesis – The Invisible Touch tour*, 02:57 – 03:29), who calls it his "first protest song." It deals with "war and chaos, written before the horrors of Yugoslavia brought strife back to central Europe and firmly onto the doorstop of the West" (Welch 2005: 68).

According to Giulia Gabrielli (in Keazor & Wübbena 2010: 91 – 96), there are four functions of a music video:

1. *"Paraphrase the verbal text of the song*: In this case, the song text has to be taken into account: images can refer to the content of the text they accompany, and they might draw directly their own character from there.
2. The central visual idea of a music video can be based on the song title.
3. *To direct the expressivity of the song by creating a specific, guiding atmosphere*. Images can bias the way the expressivity of a song is perceived, pushing its reception in the desired direction.
4. Finally images can *create matches with given parts of the song."*

'Land Of Confusion' (http://www.youtube.com/watch?v=1pkVLqSaahk) was using all four of these functions. It is "a witty video created by the Spitting Image TV puppet makers Fluck and Law [and] won them a Grammy for Best Concept Music Video" (Welch 2005: 67). The idea came as Genesis video director Jim Yukich saw on TV that "Phil Collins had already been caricatured" on the show, where his puppet was "performing the ruthlessly accurate parody "Oh, You Must Be Leaving" while weeping [...] copious tears" (Thompson 2005: 227). Spitting Image was

> "a series of satirical programmes [...] since 1984, in which lifelike but grotesque puppets act out scenes relating to topical events and people in the news, including especially politicians and members of the *royal family* [emphasis in the original]" (Room 1990: 355).

All references in the video lead back the website tvtropes.org. (cf. Music: Land of Confusion – Television Tropes and Idioms) or come from personal experience, since there exist no serious analyses as such for the video.

The video starts with "the bumbling Ronald Reagan" (Bowler & Dray 1992: 203), then president of the United States, in bed with his wife and a monkey. The monkey is a reference to the movie *Bedtime for Bonzo*, in which Reagan shared a bed with a monkey. He kisses the monkey instead of his wife (00:11) and falls asleep, starting to dream a nightmare, at which point the song starts (00:20). His wife and the monkey seem to hear the drums that "set out a staccato military tattoo" (Welch 2005: 69). The second function of a music video is fulfilled, as Reagan enters the 'Land Of Confusion' in his dreams. Between the cuts to marching people, which fulfil the fourth function of a music video, since the pictures fit to the music (especially the drums), the puppets of Banks (00:22) and Rutherford (00:25) can be seen, playing their instruments, exaggerating Banks' many keyboards that he uses onstage and Rutherford's double-neck guitar by giving it four necks. At 00:30 Collins starts singing ("I must have dreamed a thousand dreams", referring to Reagan's dream) as we see marching feet (of which he also sings, 00:40). The first function of a music video is also fulfilled, as the video paraphrases the verbal text of the song. At 00:47 Collins' puppet can be seen for the first time. It has to be noted that all of them look very ugly and the whole video is filled with black humour, which is very "British". Welch (2005: 68) thinks that the worries of this verse ("Now did you read the news today, they say the danger's gone away, but I can see the fire's still alight, burning into the night") "have a prophetic ring to them." For the line "There's too many men…" (01:03) a lot of faces can be seen. Reagan starts to sweat during his dream at 01:09. In the chorus (at 01:20) "Genesis pleaded: "This is the world we live on, these are the hands we're given. Use them and let's start trying to make it a place worth fighting for"" (Welch 2005: 69). Nancy Reagan and the monkey look out of the window and see a flying bird (01:30), which turns into a roasted chicken. Reagan seems to wake (01:37) and slips into a superman costume (01:40), while people applaud him, in order to safe the world. It fits, as the second verse (01:45) starts with the line: "Oh Superman, where are you now?" As he sings on, different (heavily guarded) persons can be seen holding speeches to a crowd of people, among them Benito Mussolini (01:45) and Ayatollah Khomeini (01:49). "The men of steel" (01:54) represent the politicians of the USSR (the steel stands for the iron curtain) and "the men of power" (01:55) represent dictators, as it might be Gaddafi, who is seen on the screens. From 02:02 to 02:35 one can see the puppet band playing, Phil Collins taking a double role as drummer and front man. At 02:40 a dinosaur stops superman Reagan from running and he falls into an armchair and watches TV, seeing Helmut Kohl (02:44), Richard Nixon (02:47), Mr. Spock (02:50) and a reporter. Musically, a new passage has started, not as aggressive as the rest and softer. Collins sings "I remember long ago, when the sun was shining and when the stars were bright, all through the night and the sound of your laughter as I held you tight…so long ago." Reagan falls asleep in his chair (03:01) and dreams of this time, the stone ages, where he lives happily with his wife. This must have been the last time when everything was innocent in the world. The sequence ends, as an animal takes away a bone, on which Reagan bites, and throws it in the air (03:33). During an instrumental interlude, the bone is parodying Kubrick's film *2001*.

As the verse begins again (03:41), Collins catches the bone and uses it as a telephone while singer Prince starts to eat his own tongue. After the line "my generation will put it right" (03:46) Pete Townsend of the band The Who can be seen on guitar. The guitar playing in the verse is influenced by Townsend's playing and the line is inspired by their song 'My Generation' (cf. Bowler & Dray 1992: 203). At 04:03, Reagan is riding in a cowboy dress on the dinosaur (another reference to his acting career, especially in Westerns) and at 04:13 Gaddafi and Margaret Thatcher can be seen on screens. The last chorus comes at 04:16 with a lot of celebrities, parodying videos like 'We Are the World' or 'Do They Know It's Christmas?' Among them are Michael Jackson and Hulk Hogan (04:33), Madonna (04:36), who has a singing mouth instead of a belly button and the pope (04:45) who plays bass. At the end of the song (04:57) Reagan wakes up again and presses the wrong button (05:15), 'Nuke' as he wants to call a 'nurse'. After an explosion (05:16) and being beaten by Nancy, the video is over.

As the whole video is full of figures from cold war and a lot of subliminal critique is given, the third function of a music video is fulfilled, too: The critique of the lyrics should be recognized and the images should help to understand the critique and exaggerate the message of the song. Tony Banks (*Tony Banks Interview from 'Genesis Songbook' DVD*, 12:26 – 12:31) jokes, that no other video "can boast all these stars, like Madonna and Prince."

Other famous music videos from the album are the video for 'Invisible Touch' (https://www.youtube.com/watch?v=pW68T84RLHw), in which the band fools around in a big hangar while playing the song or 'Throwing It All Away' (http://www.youtube.com/watch?v=xaENa3XdOAY), which shows clips of their life on tour. But then again, videos were made for all the singles from the album.

Mike Rutherford always said, that Genesis never had "their personal ultimate album" and Welch (2005: 68), who has known and followed the band from the beginning of their career, names (despite the disgust of many old Genesis fans) *Invisible Touch* as coming "closest to achieving this distinction", as "unlike many of their previous albums, there isn't one sub-standard track." Bowler & Dray (1992: 201) think that "certainly it was their best album since *Wind And Wuthering*" and "one of the very best albums of the 1980s" (92: 205). Some fan-reactions can be summed up nicely by "Alan Hewitt, founder of Genesis's official *The Waiting Room* fanzine", who "described *Invisible Touch* as the first Genesis album he ever played once and then turned into a frisbee" (Thompson 2005: 225). Ironically, the title track single of the album was dislodged off the top of the charts by Peter Gabriel's 'Sledgehammer' (cf. Bright 1988: 211), which also has one of the most elaborate videos of the 1980s.

After a five year break, in which all three of them were focussing on their solo careers and only came together as Genesis twice, first for "a short set at Atlantic Records' 40th anniversary bash on May 15, 1988" (Thompson 2005: 239) and then for the 1990 gig at Knebworth, where they played 'Mama', 'That's All', 'Throwing It All Away' and the 'Turn It On Again Medley', they came back together at the Farm for *We Can't Dance*, which would be their last studio album with Phil Collins. They did not produce it with Hugh Padgham, but with "Nick Davis, who had co-produced Tony Banks' STILL album and engineered Mike and The Mechanics' LIVING YEARS" (Platts 2007: 138). Davis can be seen in the documentary about the creation of the album 'We Can't Dance' (*Genesis-No Admittance-(1991)-Part 4*) at 1:24, when showing how the band has created 'I Can't Dance' and he became their 'house-producer' over the next years, as he was producing some of the band's solo work and remixed "Genesis' entire back catalogue" (Platts 2007: 155) for different re-issues.

With the album, they "achieved yet another blockbuster." The first three singles, " – the plaintive "No Son of Mine", the Stonesy grind of the putative title track "I Can't Dance", the sweetly balladic "Hold On My Heart" – each took up residence in the Top 20" (Thompson 2005: 244 f.). Other famous songs off the album are the hits 'Jesus He Knows Me' and 'Tell Me Why'.

Despite the inevitable hits, "the epic *Driving the Last Spike*" (Platts 2007: 139) is a "ten minute saga, [...] inspired by tales of the English navvies who built the railway network in the early 19th century" (Welch 2005: 72) and the last song 'Fading Lights', which is a long song in typical band tradition, "almost seemed as if Genesis were finally, discreetly trying to say good-bye" (Welch 2005: 71).

Platts (2007: 139) thinks that "WE CAN'T DANCE was a solid, commercial piece of work but didn't feel like a step forward for Genesis, but a rather consolidation of the formula established in the early '80s". Thompson (2005: 242) on the other hand, explains that "many of the reviews that awaited what became *We Can't Dance* were tentative, [but] they were written in the expectation of another *Invisible Touch*. Instead, *We Can't Dance* leaned more toward the *Wind and Wuthering/...And Then There Were Three* era."

The album dealt with themes such as "love in crisis, fading memories and pervading sense of sadness and anger at the ways of the world" (Welch 2005: 71). 'Jesus He Knows Me' was a satire on "the TV evangelists in the States" (Bowler & Dray 1992: 221) and 'Tell Me Why' follows Collins' critical topics from his album *...But Seriously* by being an "outburst at the problem of world hunger" (Welch 2005: 73).

Again, the videos made for the songs were highly elaborate, the most famous being 'Jesus He Knows Me', in which "Phil plays the role of American TV evangelist" (Welch 2005: 72) and 'I Can't Dance' (http://www.youtube.com/watch?v=qOyF4hR5GoE) with its famous walk. In both videos, the band is funny as ever. In the video of 'I Can't Dance' they are in the desert (00:00), waiting at an empty gas station. At 00:28 the song starts, Mike Rutherford is playing "a funky guitar" and Tony Banks pretends to drum to "the drum machine beats" (Welch 2005: 72), and at 00:51 the vocals ("Phil sings the blues", as Welch calls it) set in, while Phil has no chance to enter the car of a beautiful woman who prefers to take a reptile with her instead of him (00:59). At 01:09 the "brilliant dance routine" (Welch 2005: 72) is shown, followed by a look 'behind the scenes' as Collins sings into the mirror while they put make-up on him. At 01:31 follows the next verse, which shows the same scenario as the first verse, but this time on the beach instead of the desert and Phil has to fight against a dog (01:40) instead of a reptile. The chorus (01:49) shows the dance and he is getting his make-up again, this time on the beach. 02:15 puts the whole scenario into a bar and Phil loses his trousers to a fat man, who knows how to play pool (02:36). From 03:20 onwards, there is 'behind the scenes' material, mixed with different variations of the dance. Again, the functions of a music video are fulfilled. At 01:41 he sings about the dog, who attacks him (Feature 1: images can refer to the content of the text they accompany), at 01:49 and several other times the dance is shown, when he sings: "I can't dance..." (Feature 2: The central visual idea of a music video can be based on the song title), the atmosphere of the song ("working on a chain gang in the deep South", as Welch calls it) is expressed by the choice of the desert (00:06) as a location (feature 3: Images can bias the way the expressivity of a song is perceived, pushing its reception in the desired direction) and the scenes that are not 'behind the scenes'-material fit to feature 4: "images can *create matches with given parts of the song.*" In the live version of the following tour the beginning and the end of the song were stretched out so that Collins could celebrate the dance and was accompanied by Rutherford and Stuermer when they walked the stage (and played their instruments!). The tour was, "Mike Rutherford confessed, the most complex setup Genesis had ever taken out with it and, in some ways, the most mystifying" (Thompson 2005: 245). Memorable concerts were a concert in "Knebworth Park at the beginning of August" (Thompson 2005: 246) and "the half-dozen additional shows that were added at London's Earl's Court" (Thompson 2005: 247) in November 1992 that were "filmed and for yet another home video release and, subsequently, Genesis's first live DVD release, *The Way We Walk Live*" (Thompson 2005: 247). The focus of the tour was on more recent hits such as 'No Son of Mine', 'I Can't Dance' and 'Invisible Touch'.

The video has a nice ending: For the last walk (04:11) Collins is the last in line, stops as the others walk on and acts out a Michael Jackson parody (04:24), until Rutherford and Banks come back and take him away (04:47).

After looking at some songs and the albums from that second era, one can have a look at the list of Genesis-features and hold them up against it. Some things have changed, some have not:

- a mixture of loud passages soft passages, and musical crescendos to add to the dynamics of the arrangements (cf. 'Home by the sea', 07:53 – 09:01)
- Extended instrumental solos, electric and electronic instruments where each plays a vital role in translating the emotion of compositions which typically contain more than one mood (cf. the extended instrumental section in the live version 'Abacab' from 04:17 on)
- Very "picturesque" lyrics:

Some of them are still picturesque and storytelling (cf. 'Home by the Sea' or 'Driving the Last Spike'), but more focus on direct lyrics like love (in 'Misunderstanding' and 'Invisible Touch'); the old theme of 'Supper's Ready', the fight of bad versus evil is reappearing in 'Mama'. Criticism of society ('Land Of Confusion', 'Domino') has become a more important part. The "Englishness" still appears in songs like 'Turn It on Again' or 'Driving the Last Spike' or in their music videos; religion comes through in 'Jesus He Knows Me' and there are again cultural references (cf. the medley of 'Turn It on Again' or the Michael Jackson parody at the end of the 'I Can't Dance' video). Mythology and nature have nearly vanished, a new factor on *We Can't Dance* is the element of "fading memories and pervading sense of sadness and anger at the ways of the world."

- Visual material:
  1. Elaborate (but no more surrealistic) album covers (cf. the cover of ...*And Then There Were Three...* or their *Platinum Collection* from 2004, which collects features from different covers of their career), but also simpler, direct covers (the photo covers of the singles 'Many Too Many' and 'Turn It On Again', the colourful covers of *Abacab* or *Invisible Touch*)
  2. Elaborate stage shows (the light show on 'Home By The Sea'; the screens for 'Turn It On Again' in 1992), costumes would pop up occasionally (e.g. 'Turn It On Again' from 1984)
  3. Music videos, which appeared only in that period of the band (notable: 'Land Of Confusion', 'I Can't Dance')
- Form: Straighter structures with added instrumental sections take over instead of songs that contain of mixed bits and pieces (cf. 'Abacab', 'Home By The Sea') and simple, straight AABA-formats (cf. 'Invisible Touch')
- complex arrangements usually featuring intricate keyboard and guitar playing (cf. 'Abacab' 06:00)
- Songs with different lengths, but structured, rarely improvised: 'Turn It On Again' runs at 11:41, 'Abacab' runs at 08:52, 'Home By The Sea' runs at 12:27, opposing short songs like 'Follow You Follow Me' (03:55) and 'Misunderstanding' (03:51). Still the instrumentals of the long songs are roughly structured, but there is some room for improvising.
  - Multi-movement compositions that may or may not return to a musical theme (cf. the reprise of the chorus at the end of 'Second Home by the Sea', 11:16).
  - Rhythm & meter: Syncopations, tricky rhythms; less reliance on 4/4 time signature ('Turn It On Again' is played in 13/8)
  - Since 1980: The use of drum-machines (as in 'Mama' or 'Invisible Touch')
  - From 'Follow You Follow Me' onwards: many single hits (e.g. 'Mama', 'Invisible Touch', 'I Can't Dance' or 'Hold On My Heart')

Some things completely vanished, like the use of acoustic guitar and mellotron. It was last featured on the single 'Many Too Many' from 1978 and its loss "reflected the group's changing sound; gone was the instrument that had set so much of the mood on tracks like *Watcher of the Skies, Fountain of Salmacis* and *Dancing with the Moonlit Knight,* and had even featured prominently on A TRICK OF THE TAIL and WIND AND WUTHERING" (Platts 2007: 102).

Lyrically, some things changed as well, since mythology and nature nearly vanished. New factors came up like the use of drum-machines and an endless line of chart-topping single hits. The end of this era was reached in 1996, when "Phil Collins officially announced his departure from Genesis" (Platts 2007: 144). In the documentary about the creation of the album 'We Can't Dance' (*Genesis-No Admittance-(1991)-Part 3*), Tony Banks almost prophetically tells about the lyrics of the song 'Fading Lights' that "when you're actually experiencing the last time you ever do something, you don't know that it is the last time you ever do it" (06:03).

4.2.5   I Don't Care Anymore: Phil Collins's solo career

"I'd never really finished a song until I was on my own, in '78-'79. I just had this year of writing all these songs, basically because I was depressed, miserable..." (Phil Collins in Waller 1985: 55)

Phil Collins' first single was 'In the Air Tonight' (cf. http://www.you tube.com/watch?v=YkADj0TPrJA) from his debut album *Face Value* in 1981 and it was to become his most famous song. It starts with "a slow paced drum machine pattern" and then "gently builds up." At 00:37 he begins to sing and his "voice sustains the tension with minimal support" (Welch 2005) from other instruments. The mood of the song is described by Collins as full of "anger, hurt, bitterness, menace, and, finally, losing your temper at the end, where the drums come in" (in Thompson 2005: 181). The famous "drums crash" (Welch 2005: 108) happens at 03:16 and was to become his trademark. The drum-sound that would become typical for Phil and Genesis in the 1980s comes from producer Hugh Padgham. The two had used it when they worked with Peter Gabriel on his third album (cf. Platts 2007: 116). 'In The Air Tonight' "reached #7 in Britain, [...] the album itself topped the U.K. charts and reached #7 in America" (Platts 2007: 116). Tony Banks remembers, that "it was the biggest hit that we'd ever had [...] as a group and it was bit strange really" (*Genesis – Behind The Music Remastered,* 28:10 – 28:14). With this song, Collins "became a superstar and a millionaire many times over" (Welch 2005: 108). He himself thinks that the song "is almost, to a lot of people, what I'm about – that's what they associate me with. That's how they first heard of me. They might not have liked Genesis and suddenly there was this bloke Phil Collins who had a good single out" (Waller 1985: 122 f.). Collins' way of writing songs can be heard very nicely on a demo version from 'I Missed Again', a song from his first album (cf. *phil collins – i missed again (home demo 1980)*). It consists only of a drum machine, to which he plays along on the piano and improvises vocals. Only later the other instruments would be added.

Over the next years, he (like Banks and Rutherford) kept his solo career and his career with Genesis parallel, being successful with every album he put out, winning "cascades of awards" (Welch 2005: 110) and shaping the 80's like almost no one else did. His second album *Hello, I Must Be Going* featured the "sixties cover version" 'You Can't Hurry Love', which "became an instant success" (Waller 1985: 113). It went on with "the title track from the film *Against All Odds*", which he had left over "from the FACE VALUE era" and "which Collins reworked into a mega-hit single – a U.S. #1 and U.K. #2 hit" (Platts 2007: 130). The song got nominated for an Academy Award and Collins came to appear on shows as 'The Tonight Show', in which he even has to explain that he is still in Genesis and that this is the band he is used to be in (cf. *Phil Collins Tonight Show 1985*, 07:48).

His love for Earth, Wind and Fire included not only to work with its horn section, but also "an apparently unlikely duet with former Earth Wind and Fire vocalist Philip Bailey", which "proved there was no limit to the possibilities open to Collins" and "the softly languid "Easy Lover" (cf. http://www.youtube.com/watch?v=UFrbMfBOiYY) shot to No. 1 in Britain, No. 2 in America" (Thompson 2005: 219) in 1984. Collins calls it a "black hit and a pop hit" (Thompson 2005: 221), something that no one would connect to a progressive rock artist! Notably in the song is the guitar solo (03:05 – 03:33) played by Genesis live guitarist Daryl Stuermer. On his solo tours, "both Daryl Stuermer and Chester Thompson from the Genesis live group on guitar and drums" (Waller 1985: 119) were part of his band and just like on Genesis tours, he and Thompson would do their drum duets, "thrashing away at the drums in perfect unison" (Waller 1985: 122). He also worked with Peter Gabriel on the song "*Take Me Home*, which featured backing vocals by Peter Gabriel and Sting" (Platts 2007: 130). The song was featured on his third album *No Jacket Required* from 1985, "which stayed at number one in the UK for five weeks" (Welch 2005: 110). In a 1988 episode from the TV show 'This is your life' (*Phil Collins This Is Your Life*) one gets a good overview over his shooting star career:

- In 1988, Collins took the title role in the movie *Buster* (02:36), which deals with the great train robbery from 1963
- Snippets of Genesis and solo hits are shown (04:40)

- In 1984 he was the only one to play London and Philadelphia for the benefit concert of Live Aid due to the Concorde (06:16), which put him into the Guinness Book of Records
- His first role as an actor in 'Calamity the Cow' from 1967 (15:00)
- Of course Tony Banks and Mike Rutherford show up (15:50) and Peter Gabriel sends a message (16:59)
- Led Zeppelin's Robert Plant, with whom he recorded in 1983, sends a message (18:10)
- His charity work is mentioned (19:10), including a congratulation letter by Prince Charles
- His appearance in the cult TV show 'Miami Vice' is shown (20:33), including greetings from Philip Michael Thomas

Just as Genesis, Phil produced a lot of remarkable videos, like 'Don't Lose My Number', in which he acts out different roles in different costumes or 'Wake Up Call' (cf. http://www.youtube.com/watch?v=XwzID90zhAc), a "rousing number" (Welch 2004: 115) from 2002, in which he toys around with his past in Genesis, as a group of people follows him (02:28), asking him if "something happened on the way to heaven" (02:33), which was one his hits from the record ...*But Seriously* (co-written with Daryl Stuermer, cf. Bowler & Dray 1992: 257), crying out "All we need is a miracle!" (02:38), which refers to the hit of Mike Rutherford's band 'Mike and the Mechanics' and one guy asks: "Is Genesis getting back together?" (02:41), upon which Collins gives an irritated look and walks off.

Collins' songs deal with different topics. The most frequent one is love as for example in 'I Missed Again', which features "a brass section" and "was Phil's first solo hit in the US" (Welch 2005: 109). The song was "written during the break of his first marriage" (Welch 2005: 108). He also criticized society, for example in 'That's Just the Way It Is', "a number Collins wrote in response to the ongoing conflict in Northern Ireland" (Thompson 2005: 237), which in a way also deals with religion. The song featured also David Crosby on backing vocals and was from the album ...*But Seriously* from 1989, which "was the fastest selling album in UK history" (Welch 2005: 110). It reflects an "aching regret for things past" (Welch 2005: 110) on a song like 'All Of My Life' and heavy criticism on the hit single 'Another Day in Paradise' (the song and its video deal with the "concerns of the homeless") with it's "simple keyboard theme, a handclapping back beat" (Welch 2005: 111) or 'Colours', a song "which points up hunger, poverty, and the lack of human rights" (Welch 2005: 111). The song broke with Collins's typical short verse-refrain-verse-refrain-scheme (e.g. 'Easy Lover' and 'Wake up Call'). Following ...*But seriously* he went on the highly successful 'Serious Tour' in 1990. Apart from "Daryl and Chester from Genesis" his famous live band included "the Phenix Horns, Leland Sklar on bass and Brad Cole on keyboards, plus the Seriousettes, three backing singers" (Bowler & Dray 1992: 214). Apart from new hits like 'Another Day In Paradise', on which he played keyboards onstage and collected money for "the Coalition for Temporary Shelter" (Thompson 2005: 236) and other songs from ...But Seriously, he gave great live renditions of older songs like 'In The Air Tonight' and more unknown songs like 'Hand In Hand' from Face Value (cf. Welch 2005: 109).

Occasionally he would also still write "storytelling" lyrics as e.g. 'Driving Me Crazy' from his album Testify from 2002, which "is an almost frantic declaration of obsessive love" (Welch 2005: 115). On his album covers, his face was seen most of the time, a collection of these made out the cover of his compilation Hits from 1998, which "shot to number one in the UK charts and was number 18 in the US." A year later, Collins "provided the songs for Disney"'s animated version of Tarzan, and won an Academy Award for his efforts", its most successful song being "the tuneful hit single You'll Be in my Heart" (Platts 2007: 150). In 2004/05 he went on the "First Final Farewell Tour" (cf. Platts 2007: 153), which should mark an end to his busy touring life. Today, his success has made him more famous as a solo artist than as a member of Genesis.

5. Fading Lights: from 1997 onwards

After Collins' departure, Banks and Rutherford kept working. They had written songs and hired "a new singer: Ray Wilson, born in 1968", who had been known "as the lead vocalist of Stiltskin" (Platts 2007: 144). They released one album, *Calling All Stations*, which "entered the chart at No.2" in Britain, but in America only peaked at "No. 54" (Thompson 2005: 268).

The title track "has a pessimistic yet defiant tone" (Welch 2005: 76), that was observant all over the album and Phil Collins' direct and driving approach was clearly missed. The first single from the album, 'Congo', "breached the Top 30" (Thompson 2005: 268) in Britain. The next single, 'Shipwrecked' did not chart. The album's dark, sombre tone is lifted during 'The Dividing Line', where Wilson's voice "recalls Peter Gabriel" (Welch 2005: 78). Videos were made for 'Congo', 'Shipwrecked' and 'Not about Us'.

The critiques were harsh, the *NMW* saying that "the world doesn't care enough about Genesis to make the effort" to buy the album and "like the rest of the population, they've forgotten why they were once any good" (Platts 2007: 145). *Q* wrote that the album consists of "just darkness, confusion, individual isolation" and described it as "one-paced and one-dimensional" (Platts 2007: 145). The band toured in Europe with Wilson singing great versions of old Genesis classics by Gabriel as well as newer songs (cf. Thompson 2005: 269), but due to the bad charting of the album in America, the American shows of the tour had to be cancelled (cf. Platts 2007: 146).

After the tour no new albums were recorded. Genesis has been kept alive by "tribute bands and compilation albums" (Welch 2005: 76) and sometimes rumours of reunions were being spread, especially when "on May 11, 1998, past and present Genesis members reunited briefly at Heathrow Airport to promote the release of the ARCHIVE set" and "Tony Banks, Peter Gabriel, Anthony Phillips, John Silver, Phil Collins, Steve Hackett and Mike Rutherford all gathered together for the first time, were filmed and posed for photographs" (Platts 2007: 149). In "September 2000, although it was a private performance […] in honor of the band's longtime manager Tony Smith", Banks, Collins, Rutherford and Stuermer "performed a four-song set" acoustically, while "Peter Gabriel attended the event in a non-performing capacity" (Platts 2007: 152). "July 2001 saw the release of […] a 100-minute documentary" on DVD, which showed "Collins and Banks performing *Afterglow*" (Platts 2007: 153). Apart from that and the already mentioned 1999 version of 'The Carpet Crawlers', nothing serious happened until 2007, when "Banks, Collins and Rutherford were indeed reuniting as Genesis to play a series of stadium concerts in Europe in the summer of 2007, to be followed by U.S. dates later in the year" (Platts 2007: 155). The tour of course also featured Chester Thompson and Daryl Stuermer and started in Helsinki on July 15, 2007 and the setlist covered all of Genesis' history, as it included songs from all eras, like 'Turn It on Again', 'Tonight Tonight Tonight', 'Invisible Touch', 'Throwing It All Away', a drum duet (beginning on two stools!) by Thompson and Collins, 'I Know What I Like' (including Phil's tambourine dance) or 'The Carpet Crawlers' (cf. Platts 2007: 157). The European leg of the tour ended with a free concert in Circus Maximus in Rome, released on DVD and Blu Ray as *When in Rome*.

5.1   Out Into the Daylight: Mike Rutherford's solo career

> The renewed success of the band [Mike + the Mechanics] has undoubtedly been heart-warming for Mike Rutherford, who like Collins and Gabriel has been able to enjoy more than one career during a lifetime of achievement. (Welch 2005: 123)

Mike Rutherford released his first solo record, *Smallcreep's Day*, "in February 1980". It "charted at #13 in Britain" and for the album, "Rutherford enlisted Anthony Phillips to play keyboards" (Platts 2007: 107). He released another one, *Acting very strange*, "in early 1982" (Platts 2007: 126) and handled the vocals himself. "Among the album's musicians" was Genesis live guitarist Daryl Stuermer. The album "reached #23 in the U.K., but [like its predecessor] didn't take off in North America" (Platts 2007: 126).

In 1985, he founded the band 'Mike and the Mechanics, which "featured gifted singers Paul Carrack (ex-Ace and Squeeze) and Paul Young (from Manchester's Sad Café)" (Welch 2005: 122). The band was taken by America "to its heart, with 'Silent Running' becoming a major hit single there" (Bowler & Dray 1992: 197 f.). The other big hit from the album was 'All I Need Is A Miracle', which "reached #26 in the U.S." (Platts 2007: 131). The success went on with the second album *The Living Years*, "which peaked at number two in the UK" (Welch 2005: 123) and Rutherford became, after his frontmen Collins and Gabriel, the most successful member of Genesis. Like with Gabriel and Collins, who seemed to be more successful in their solo careers, some "young fans of Mike & the Mechanics had no idea that 'Mike' was connected with a legendary rock band their parents listened to in the Seventies" (Welch 2005: 122). Apart from

Rutherford and his two singers, the band consisted of "Adrian Lee and Peter Van Hooke" (Bowler & Dray 1992: 197) on keyboards and drums. In 1988, guitarist Tim Renwick was added to the group (cf. Thompson 2005: 238). Rutherford wrote a lot of songs together with "Christopher Neil and B.A. Robertson" (Welch 2005: 122).

The band carried on successfully in the 1990s. Chris Welch (2005: 123) thinks the song 'A Time And A Place' from their third album *Word Of Mouth* from 1991 can "easily match anything produced by colleagues Collins or Gabriel." After the making of their album *Mike and the Mechanics* a.k.a. *M6*, singer Paul Young died surprisingly "in July 2000, aged 53" (Welch 2005: 124). Rutherford and Carrack released one more album together, *Rewired* "in July 2004" (Thompson 2005: 282), before Carrack left the band as well and Rutherford kept changing the line-up of the Mechanics for the next years.

On his first solo record, Rutherford sounds, according to Welch (2005: 121) like "mid-Seventies Genesis." It is "a semiconcept album" (Thompson 2005: 169), one side featured the 'Smallcreep's Day Suite', a long piece in the tradition of Genesis (cf. Platts 2007: 107). On his next album, he drifted away from his first band and with Mike and the Mechanics, he had found his style by creating "fresh, radio-friendly pop songs" (Rutherford in Thompson 2005: 223). Their first single, 'Silent Running' was accompanied by a video (cf. http://www.youtube.com/watch?v=ttJsuLmcmiY), which includes film sequences. The song represents the radio-friendliness structure pretty good: It starts with a keyboard intro until 00:56, in 01:10 Paul Carrack sings the chorus. At 01:25 the verse starts, at 01:53 the chorus starts again. The verse follows at 02:24, the chorus at 02:53, followed by a guitar solo from Rutherford from 03:23 – 03:53, when the verse sets in again. At 04:21 the chorus follows and runs until the end. Tony Banks (in Platts 2007: 131) thought that Rutherford "diluted himself quite a lot" with this kind of music.

The Mechanics' lyrics dealt with different topics. Another big hit, 'The Living Years' (cf. http://www.youtube.com/watch?v=APXwdkdhC2c) includes "a touching lyric about a father and son relationship" (Welch 2005: 122). It has a similar structure to 'Silent Running', just like 'Over My Shoulder' (cf. http://www.youtube.com/watch?v=tKiLGysBO7U), which deals with the simple topic of love. It "made a glorious adornment to the U.K. charts as it flew to No. 12 in February 1995" (Thompson 2005: 257). It was one of the last successful 'Genesis'-member numbers for a while and Rutherford (2007: 315) thought that "The Mechanics had somehow managed to slip through with the 'Over My Shoulder' song, but after that, the door came down."

Their album covers had an extraordinary style (cf. *M6*), sometimes featuring the shown mechanic. With this band, Mike Rutherford created a second band that sounded hardly like his first one, allowing him to play different music and work with different people. Up until today, Mike and the Mechanics are touring all over the world.

5.2   Man of spells: Tony Banks' solo career

> I think the main reason Tony didn't have much success as a solo artist was because he wasn't a singer by profession. Audiences can generally relate to a voice much more than they can relate to an instrument. (youtube-user jhillst's comment on the video of 'For A While')

Despite his criticism on Rutherford's own band, Tony Banks "has released a succession of well made solo albums over the years, most reflecting his desire to create commercially acceptable rock/pop music rather than celebrate his skills as a virtuoso keyboard player" (Welch 2005: 119). His first solo album, *A Curious Feeling*, was "released in 1979" and just like Mike Rutherford's solo record of that time "a concept album" (Platts 2007: 107). The only other musician on the record was "Genesis drummer Chester Thompson" (Welch 2005: 119) and Banks himself "played keyboards, guitar and bass" (Platts 2007: 119), which he was not used to do, so sometimes "Chester coached him through the bass playing" (Bowler & Dray 1992: 157). The vocals "were delivered by Kim Beacon, once of String Driven Thing", as can be heard on the song 'For a While', (cf. http://www.you tube.com/watch?v=VRz7ZByNC58) which "was issued as a single but without chart success" (Welch 2005: 119). It has a simple structure and the topic is the topic of love.

The length of the song is 03:28, starts with a guitar intro until 00:15 when Beacon starts to sing the verse, followed by the chorus at 01:14. The verse comes at 01:36, then the chorus at 02:07 until 02:56 when the guitar from the intro comes back and finishes the song off. The song is kept very simple and ripples along.

On his next album *The Fugitive* (featuring among others Daryl Stuermer on guitar, cf. Thompson 2005: 209), Banks decided "to take the lead vocals himself" (Thompson 2005: 209). On this album it seems that Banks "could not find the right niche between his classical leanings and pop aspirations" (Welch 2005: 119). As a single he released 'This Is Love', "a classic pop tune" that "failed to get any radio play, presumably because of DJs' preconceptions" (Bowler & Dray 1992: 184). Nonetheless, "*This is Love* did sneak into the Top 20 in Poland" (Platts 2007: 127).

In 1986 he "released the SOUNDTRACKS album" (Platts 2007: 135), which saw him working with singer "Toyah Wilcox (Mrs. Robert Fripp)" (Thompson 2005: 223) and yet another vocalist, "Scots singer Fish, formerly front man of the group Marillion" (Welch 2005: 119), with whom he wrote 'Shortcut to Somewhere', a song that was accompanied by a funny, slapstick music video. The parallels between Genesis and Marillion are very interesting. In their beginnings they were compared with "old" Genesis, as Banks remembers: "...they had a No. 1 album [...], taking ideas that we'd used on *Foxtrot*, when *Foxtrot* was not a big seller at all. It was more the keyboard player than anyone and the fact that Fish's voice obviously sounds a bit like Peter's" (Thompson 2005: 181). Fish also had a "penchant for lengthy, wordy epics of abstruse mythology, anecdote, and incident" (Thompson 2005: 180). Holm-Hudson (2008: 143) sees the music of the early Genesis "and especially *The Lamb*" as a "touchpoint for neo-progressive rock, the most commercially successful example being Marillion." The band would face the same "dilemma" as Genesis in their later years: Their career is divided by critics and fans into two eras, the first being "up to the point Fish left the band for a solo career in 1988", the second beginning "with new lead singer Steve Hogarth" (Hegarty & Halliwell 2012: 188). The combination of Fish/Banks sounds promising and might remind some fans of the old Genesis, but unfortunately the album was only "peaking at #75 in Britain" (Platts 2007: 135).

At the same time, Mike Rutherford became very successful with his band Mike and the Mechanics, which lead Banks to the idea to form a "group called Bankstatement, whose self-titled album was released in August 1989" (Platts 2007: 135). There are also some references to Phil Collins' solo career, as there are "the powerful Phantom Horns who ride into the opening track 'Throwback' with all trumpets blowing" (Welch 2005: 120). The album's "emphasis on pop songs and ballads, as opposed to vast orchestral scores and keyboard passages" led to the result that the band "was all but ignored by fans and record buyers alike" (Thompson 2005: 238). Disappointed, Banks dissolved the band and in the 1990s released solo records under his name, but with different vocalists. The "critics were kinder" but Banks "still failed to ignite the charts" (Welch 2005: 120).

As an example, a song like 'Red Day on Blue Street' (http://www.youtube.com/watch?v=sy6PNg5Nt-U) is quite different from his work with Fish. It is written by Banks and "pop star Nik Kershaw" (Welch 2005: 120), who also sings it and described by Jackson as "a perfect blend of both Nik Kershaw and Tony Banks." The song begins with a "very rhythmic and electronic pulsating, much like the best of Kershaw's solo work" (Jackson, n.d.). With a length of almost six minutes, it seems "perhaps a tad long for this kind of pop song" (Gerhardts, n.d.). Lyrically, "the red and blue refers to political parties in England", where "Labour is red and Conservative is blue" (McMahan 1998: 383).

It shows that, "as a personality he [Banks] remains in the background, which is not helped by the variety of singers he has used over the years" (Bowler & Dray 1992: 215). That made him to "a fairly faceless individual when it comes to solo work" (Bowler & Dray 1992: 184). Banks himself got a little frustrated, when "people don't realize I do anything between Genesis albums" and he is being asked "'What have you been doing while Phil and Mike have been on top of the charts?'" (Platts 2007: 136). Thompson (2005: 170) explains that in his solo work "elements of Genesis, then, lurk everywhere, but [...] own innate originality is never compromised" and Tony Smith, manager of the band since 1973 (cf. Dodd 2007: 333) thinks that this "simply reminded us that, no matter what else the band did, it would be nothing without Banks."

After one last album in 1995, *Strictly Inc.* (cf. Platts 2007: 142), his failure as a solo artist made him "move away from writing pop material and instead [he] concentrated on composing classical themes", the first one being the "album Seven [...] released in 2004 on which the London Philharmonic Orchestra performed his 'Suite for Orchestra'" (Welch 2005: 120).

This was something that "the original group's most devout admirers have dreamed of for so many years" (Thompson 2005: 283) and Platts (2007: 154) thinks that the album "seemed to fulfil something only hinted at in the classical leanings of his best earlier work" with Genesis. Banks had found his niche and released the album's sequel *Six: Pieces for Orchestra* in 2012 (cf. Eddins). In an interview from 2012 (*Tony Banks Interview May 1, 2012*), he explains that for example the composition 'Blade' "recalls [...] songs like 'The Cinema Show', I think it recalls this kind of attitude" (06:50). A composition like 'Siren' (http://www.youtube.com/watch?v=Xl23zqz79bQ) sound much more like Banks' epic keyboard compositions and bares much more his style than the attempted pop songs he wrote during his solo career. With its length of 08:53 it goes back to the long songs.

As for Banks' album covers, they were kept relatively simple, on most of them his face can be seen or there are photographs. *Seven* shows a drawing of a landscape.

Phil Collins (in *Tony Banks Interview from 'Genesis: A History'*, 06:27 – 06:46) sums up Tony's solo career very nicely:

> "Tony, I would say, is the most important writer in Genesis. [...] Him, with Mike as a closed second, the most important writers in Genesis in terms about what people like about Genesis and yet, Tony has the least success. But if people knew what he brought into Genesis, they'd probably give his solo work more of a listen."

6. Against All Odds: Conclusion

> Speaking of names for things, Confucius pointed out that when terms are not well defined, discussion is smooth. (Haynes 2007: 13)

Having looked at the evolution of the band throughout the years, separating the different eras and taking a short glimpse at each member's solo career, one can take the 'Genesis-feature'-list one last time to see what has changed, what has remained and who had influenced which part of the band's trademark. The main focus is on the division between the two "eras", era 1 (E1) stands for the time Peter Gabriel was singer, era 2 (E2) stands for the time with Phil Collins as frontman. For each era there will be selected songs as examples for certain trademarks.

- **A mixture of loud passages, soft passages, and musical crescendos to add to the dynamics of the arrangements**
Passages from 'Supper's Ready' (E1), passages from 'Home by the Sea/Second Home by the Sea' (E2); Solo: Hackett's 'Ace of Wands', Banks' 'Siren'
- **Extended instrumental solos, electric and electronic instruments where each plays a vital role in translating the emotion of compositions which typically contain more than one mood**
'Supper's ready' (E1), the extended instrumental section in 'Abacab' (E2); Solo: Hackett's 'Ace of Wands'
- **Acoustic versus electric sections**
The intro of 'The Musical Box' and 'Lover's Leap' from 'Supper's ready' (E1), the song 'Entangled' (E2); Solo: Hackett's 'Nomads'
- **Lyrics:**
Mythology: 'The Musical Box' (E1), 'Squonk' (E2); Solo: Hackett's 'Narnia', Phillips's 'We're all as we lie'
Nature: 'How Dare I Be So Beautiful?' (E1), 'Ripples' (E2)
Religious lyrics: 'Supper's ready' (E1), 'One for the Vine' (E2); Solo: Phillips's 'Magdalen', Gabriel's 'Blood of Eden', Collins' 'That's Just the Way It is'
"Englishness": 'Willow Farm' (E1), 'Blood on the rooftops' (E2); Solo: Hackett's 'Carry on Up the Vicarage'
Psychological themes: The whole album *The Lamb Lies down on Broadway* (E1), 'Entangled' (E2)

Storytelling lyrics: 'The Musical Box' (E1), 'Driving the Last Spike' (E2); Solo: Hackett's 'Carry on Up the Vicarage', Phillips' 'Birdsong', Collins' 'Driving Me Crazy', Rutherford's 'The Living Years', Gabriel's 'Moribund the Burgermeister'

Cultural references: The citation of The Rolling Stones in 'It' (E1), the live Medley of 'Turn It On Again' (E2)

Protest/critical lyrics: 'The Knife' (E1), 'Land Of Confusion' (E2); Solo: Gabriel's 'Biko', Collins' 'That's Just the Way It Is', Rutherford's 'Silent Running', Banks' 'Red Day on Blue Street'

Love: 'Invisible Touch' (E2); Solo: Hackett's 'Can't Let Go', Phillips' 'God if I saw her now', Gabriel's 'Modern Love', Collins' 'I Missed Again', Rutherford's 'Over My Shoulder', Banks' 'For a While'

- **Visual material:**

Elaborate album covers: the covers of all the Gabriel era albums from *Trespass* on (E1), *...And Then There Were Three...*, the *Platinum Collection* (E2); Solo: Phillips' *The Geese and the ghost*, Hackett's *Please Don't Touch*, Gabriel's single *No Self Control*, Rutherford's *M6*, Banks' *A Curious Feeling*

Elaborate stage shows: the costumes of Gabriel (E1), the lights in 'Supper's Ready' from 1976; the screens for 'Turn It On Again'; 'costumes' of Collins on some occasions (E2); Solo: Gabriel's costumes (*Peter Gabriel Plays Live*); another important factor is the storytelling, which both of them (Gabriel before 'Supper's Ready', Collins before 'Home By The Sea') were doing

(Elaborate) music videos: 'Land Of Confusion', 'I Can't Dance' (E2); Solo: Gabriel's 'Solsbury Hill', Collins' 'Wake up Call', Rutherford's 'The Living Years', Banks' 'For a While'

Photographs as album covers: their first album *From Genesis to Revelation*, *The Lamb Lies Down On Broadway* (E1), the singles *Many Too Many, Turn it On Again* (E2); Solo: Gabriel's *Peter Gabriel Plays Live*, Collins' *...But Seriously*, Rutherford's *Acting Very Strange*, Banks' *Soundtracks*

- **Form:**

Unconventional forms: 'Supper's ready' (E1), 'Home by the Sea/Second Home by the Sea' (E2); Solo: Hackett's 'Ace of Wands'

Simple structure: 'I Know What I Like' (E1), 'Misunderstanding' (E2); Solo: Gabriel's 'Biko', Collins' 'Wake up Call', Rutherford's 'Over My Shoulder', Banks' 'For a While'

- **Complex arrangements usually featuring intricate keyboard and guitar playing:**

Banks' keyboard solo in 'Apocalypse in 9/8' and Hackett's guitar playing in 'The Musical Box' (E1), the instrumental section of 'Abacab' (E2); Solo: Hackett's 'Every Day'

- **Song lengths:**

Long songs: 'The Musical Box' & 'Supper's ready' (E1), 'Abacab', 'Home By The Sea/Second Home By The Sea' (E2); Solo: Phillips' 'Aboretum Suite'

Short songs: 'The Lamb Lies Down On Broadway' (E1), 'Invisible Touch' (E2); Solo: Collins' 'Easy Lover'

- **The use of Mellotron**

The intro to 'Watcher of the skies' (E1), the solo in 'Entangled' (E2)

- **Multi-movement compositions that may or may not return to a musical theme. In some cases the end section may bear little resemblance to the first part of the song.**

The end of 'Supper's ready' takes up the first part 'Lover's Leap' and repeats it (E1), the reprise of the chorus at the end of 'Second Home by the Sea' (E2); Solo: The interlude section from Hackett's 'Every Day'

- **Rhythm & meter: Syncopations, tricky rhythms; less reliance on 4/4 time signature**

'Apocalypse in 9/8' (E1), 'Turn It on Again' (E2); Solo: Gabriel's 'Solsbury Hill', Hackett's 'Ace of Wands'

- **The use of drum-machines**

'Mama', 'I Can't Dance', 'Invisible Touch' (E2); Solo: Collins's 'In the Air Tonight'

- **Single hits**

'I Know What I like' (E1), 'Follow You Follow Me' 'Turn It on Again', 'Tonight Tonight Tonight' 'Invisible Touch', 'I Can't Dance' (E2); Solo: Gabriel's 'Solsbury Hill', Collins' 'In the Air Tonight', Rutherford's 'Silent Running'

- **Concept albums**

   The Lamb Lies Down On Broadway (E1); Solo: Phillips' *Twelve*, Rutherford's *Smallcreep's Day*, Banks' *A Curious Feeling*

So, one can see that most of the things that Genesis fans of the first era used to love, be it musically or lyrically, were carried on in the second era. Some things that the three-men-line-up has been blamed for (e.g. the writing of short songs, simplicity of lyrics) have already appeared in the five-men-era. One can also see the different influences, when bringing in songs from the solo career. The progressive-rock-features that made out the band's early years, were mainly reappearing in Steve Hackett's (and to some extent in Anthony Phillip's) solo career. Although it seems that Tony Banks and Mike Rutherford had bigger influence on song writing during the time as a foursome, Steve Hackett had quiet a big impact on the sound of the music, as one can hear when listening to his solo albums. He creates a romantic atmosphere, something that only Tony Banks would now continue in Genesis and that logically became weaker. The storytelling went with him and the cover artwork changed after he left.

The music that shaped Genesis, nevertheless, has always been a product of the improvisation between Banks, Collins and Rutherford, be it 'Supper's Ready' or 'Invisible Touch'. Collins sums it up: "Providing the majority of members are still original members, you've still got whatever it is – the chemistry, the identifiable sound or style – it's still there" (Waller 1985: 129). And manager Tony Smith (2007: 332) agrees that jamming and improvisation were "a major part of how they wrote." He also thinks (in *Genesis – When In Rome – Come Rain Or Shine HD*, 07:54), that the chemistry of the three together "is so different from anything they can do individually." So all the parts of the solo careers put together create what is the basis for Genesis.

Peter Gabriel was still very keen on the visuals in his whole career and Genesis themselves were not less visual-oriented after he left. They just moved with time and success (i.e. bigger venues) from costumes to extraordinary light shows and big screens. Phil Collins, who gets blamed for turning Genesis into a pop-band with hit singles, of course had enormous solo success with that same recipe, but was not the only one: Mike and the Mechanics were just as "poppy" and radio-friendly and Peter Gabriel released hit-single after hit-single. Tony Banks tried as well and seemed to have learned only later that his strength was not the short pop format, but the classical, long structures that he was famous for in Genesis. When writing together with Rutherford and Collins, the three would complement each other, writing epics as well as pop hits.

Lyrically, it were also the two guitarists, Hackett and Phillips, who carried on progressive rock's and early Genesis's topics like mythology and the "Englishness" as well as the storytelling, something that (surprisingly?) was also featured in Collins' solo career. The topics of criticism and religion were used by Gabriel, Collins, Banks and Rutherford, and love, the topic that everyone assumed Collins was master of, was used by everyone (yes, even Peter Gabriel writes love songs).

When it comes to the loss of some instruments as trademarks, Genesis is not to blame as well. It is just a natural process as technology advanced. Thompson (2005: 187) is of the opinion that from 1980 onwards,

> "many of Genesis's most recognizable traits – the delicate 12-string guitars, the Yamaha CP 70 electric piano, the Mellotron – would be pushed away as Banks, in particular, replenished his arsenal with the new technology, [...], at exactly the same time as every other keyboard player made the same transitions."

Are we any wiser now? The reputation of the band should be rethought by many fans that ought to be more open. They call themselves 'progressive rock' fans and Genesis did exactly what the word 'progressive' implies. Even in their first era, they progressed from one album to another, avoiding prog-rock clichés after *Foxtrot*. The features of progressive rock that are collected by Jerry Luck and John J. Sheinbaum in chapter 2 are what became the frame of the genre, and if a band broke out of this frame, it was criticized and banned by the fans. Another factor was that progressive rock is a very 'elitist' genre and its fans (in Genesis' case the so-called "Genesis Freaks", cf. Platts 2007: 28) do not like to share their favourite bands with the public. So hit singles are something they are not terribly fond of. The whole genre seems paradox when thinking about that.

Genesis, however, did not stick to the rules and did as the word said: They progressed and one can clearly see which member brought in which influence and how the music developed and changed, when the line-up changed. Phil Collins, being most critical about the fans' reactions, sees his own influence by the different background, saying to the *Rolling Stone* in 1983 that

> "Genesis only began to break when the lyrics became less story-oriented. The basic difference between me and Pete and Tony and Mike is that lyrically they're a bit emotionally screwed up. They went to boarding school all their lives, only saw their families on holidays, while I went to regular school, went home every day" (Platts 2007: 128).

Even Steve Hackett admits, that he "found that all the guys in the band were often very resistant to showing their feelings" (Fielder 1984: 55). Collins adds (in Thompson 2005: 224) that

> "I don't dominate Genesis. It's just that since *Duke*, I've become an equal third. To those that wish I'd go back to being subservient to Mike and Tony, well, we're all changing. [...] We were always a group of songwriters who would write 3-, 10- and 20-minute songs. We still write 10-minute songs, like 'Domino', but unfortunately, the three-minute songs have gotten better and become hits. I don't feel we've bastardized the way we were, as we still

work the same way. Diehard fans will say, 'Rubbish. "The Carpet Crawlers", "I Know What I Like" – that was progressive!' But I don't see that. We'd have killed for hit singles back in the early days!"

Live guitarist Daryl Stuermer (in Platts 2007: 110) thinks that drummer Chester Thompson and him had "influenced the group's sound as well", especially when they played with Phil on his solo tours, who was surrounded by American musicians, whom "he was a big fan of […], so he was bringing that in with the British music." He interprets the changed sound as "the music getting tighter and more sophisticated. Maybe it was more 'pop', but the band got better musically, the musicianship got better" (Platts 2007: 140). Thompson is of the opinion, that "the music's evolved a lot. A lot of old fans would argue and say they can't do this or that but I think it's a sign of maturity" (Fielder 1984: 121). He admits that "some of their older stuff was really quite advanced for its time" and that "they now say in five minutes what used to take them fifteen minutes" and confirms that "there's some magic that happens when the three of them [Banks, Collins, Rutherford] get together." Thompson himself had played, previously to Genesis, with very different bands like "Frank Zappa" or "Weather Report – one of Phil Collin's all-tome favourite groups" (Waller 1985: 48) and Daryl Stuermer "had spent several years working with Jean-Luc Ponty" (Bowler & Dray 1992: 151). Collins even thinks that despite the different musical and cultural background, Thompson "understood a lot of the material better than Bill [Bruford] had done" (Fielder 1984: 99). About his own playing Collins explains that "with early Genesis, I wanted to show everybody I could play. […] And when I listen back to Genesis, I find that there are songs where I should have laid back a little more" (Waller 1985: 151) and adds that "once you've learned how to use odd times in your music you no longer need to prove to yourself that you can" (Thompson 2005: 214). And Tony Banks explains, "we've been such a slow growing band but we never stopped growing since the moment we started" (Waller 1985: 127). He also thinks that the solo records provided "new input" and that "each time you come back and make a new album, you're bringing new ideas in" (in Genesis – No Admittance-(1991)-Part 2, 09:49).

So is Collins to 'blame' for becoming an equal third? How would the band have carried on if he had left and Gabriel would have formed the three-men-line-up with Banks and Rutherford, with Hackett and his progressive music all gone? Would it have been 'Sledgehammer' by Genesis that was on top of the charts instead of being a Gabriel solo number? Would fans have moaned for the drummer that had played all these tricky rhythms and kept them progressive or would they have still seen Gabriel as the "Prog-God"? Another thing that should always be kept in mind is that, in spite of all the prejudices, all of the members have always been and have remained friends and helped each other on their individual records. Especially Gabriel and Collins "became close friends" (Waller 1985: 35) and played on each other's solo albums. Their way of working when writing solo records was also the same. As Gabriel describes in *Peter Gabriel on The South Bank Show 1983, Making of Security*, he "starts improvising" on the piano once he has "his rhythms locked into the drum machine" (12:07). Collins works the same way, singing to "mainly just keyboards for the melodies, with the rhythm maintained by a Roland drum-machine" (Waller 1985: 61), as can be heard on the demo for 'I Missed Again'. Funnily enough, they were sharing some other similarities over the years: Collins' world tour from 1997 had a round stage in the middle of the hall as well as Gabriel's world tour from 2003 (cf. Thompson 2005: 277). They even started to look alike and both were wearing the same kind of clothes when looking at live videos from 2003 (Gabriel) and 2004 (Collins). In the documentary *Come Rain Or Shine*, Collins explains at 30:30 that "Tony and Mike together are more the spirit of Genesis than me. [...] People just don't know, they just think the singer is the guy that does it all. [...] That's always been the problem. They thought Peter Gabriel did it all. And it really wasn't that way." After having looked at the list and the different careers, people should really rethink their opinions that the band was only driven on by their two singers, especially as they both deny it! Collins (2007: 170) also points out that he was never given a hard time by the fans when he took over. Quite the contrary, they wanted "their band [...] to survive and so they gave us every encouragement." Rutherford (2007: 169) thinks "because he was inhouse, so people knew him, and he had sung a bit on stage before, [so] the audiences wanted to like him; they wanted it to work." So the "bashing" of "new" Genesis and Collins in special was to come much later – one might wonder when exactly it started!

Daryl Stuermer, "who never appears on Genesis albums" (Waller 1985: 124) played on solo records of Banks, Collins and Rutherford. When reading some comments by youtube-users, Stuermer gets blamed for destroying Steve Hackett's guitar melodies. He himself explains that he "was never given a hard time, but [...] expected it", because "Steve definitely did have a following and an original style of playing" (Fielder 1984: 103). When meeting for the first time, Hackett said: "Daryl Stuermer, you're my second favourite guitarist in the world!" Tony Banks thinks that Stuermer is "so versatile he gave us another strength" (Banks 2007: 201) and that "he added excitement because he could play very fast and extremely in time" (Banks 2007: 208). Especially a song like 'Firth of Fifth', although being one of Hackett's most famous guitar melodies, became much more powerful when played by Stuermer. He admits that "I've duplicated some things, and on others I've put in my own little riffs", because "some of the material sounded dated anyway" (Fielder 1984: 103). It is a shame that he gets blamed for it by some, because Bruce Haynes (2007: 88) rightly writes, that "some parts of a piece are automatically altered every time it is played" and that even "two consecutive performances of a piece by the same player that use the same instrument and notes" can vary every time.

Tony Banks agrees that "we were at our strongest live, because we not only had Daryl, we also had Chester Thompson on drums" (Banks 2007: 201). Chester Thompson played drums with Tony Banks and Phil Collins. The other members also kept playing with each other. Collins and Rutherford both played with Hackett and Phillips. Gabriel played with Phillips, Collins and Rutherford on his first solo sessions. They all remained friends as was shown in the 1982 reunion concert, where the band helped Peter Gabriel after the WOMAD festival.

Another factor is that "there is a lot of humour in Genesis that gets overlooked" (Collins in Waller 1985: 128), a humour that can be found in many songs and videos and does not correspond with the 'elitist', serious genre of progressive rock. Early songs like 'I Know What I Like', 'Willow Farm' or especially 'Harold the Barrel' (by Russell 2004: 80) from *Nursery Cryme* are compared to the humour of *Monty Python*. When the band met in 1998 at Heathrow, "Tony Banks delighted the entire gathering when, standing as if to offer a toast, he instead announced "We managed to sack the lot of you."" (Thompson 2005: 272).

Also the role of the producers should be taken into account. Peter Gabriel, Phil Collins and Genesis all shared the same producer – Hugh Padgham – in the 1980s and he played an important role during the creation of their albums.

Some of the author's of the cited books have tried to pin it down themselves. By the time punk rock had overcome progressive rock, Steve Hackett had left the band "and the three remaining members of Genesis were veering towards album-oriented rock (AOR)", as Hegarty & Halliwell (2011: 181) call it. They point out correctly, that Peter Gabriel, in his solo career, also developed "a departure from progressive rock" (2011: 223). As for Genesis, they write that the band had

> "reinvented themselves as pop versions of progressive rock, in different ways and for different lengths of time, taking the rich layering of progressive rock and epic development and condensing them into shorter

rock or pop songs. By the mid-1980s, Genesis had become the most commercially successful of these bands and had a string of US number one singles" (Hegarty & Halliwell 2011: 223).

Robin Platts (2007: 118 f.) summarizes that "between Steve Hackett's departure and the release of ABACAB [...] Genesis had become a fundamentally different group from the one that had captured the imaginations of fans in the Gabriel years and even the A TRICK OF THE TAIL/WIND & WUTHERING era." He adds, that

> "whether nor not the band made a conscious effort to become more commercial is open to speculation. In all likelihood, their increased success in the single charts was really a byproduct of their move towards shorter songs, a simpler sound and more personal, straightforward lyrics."

He compares them to The Beatles by naming their albums *Please Please Me* and *Sgt. Pepper*: "The brand name is the same, but it's almost like comparing two different groups." The Beatles were celebrated for their quick development, for their new ideas and for the fact that no album sounded like the one before. The Beatles were pioneers for the genre of progressive rock and the whole era of music in general, but not many bands were doing it their way, many rested on their laurels once they were established. Dave Thompson (2005: 255) explains that "Bands can, and do, exist in abeyance. The Rolling Stones, for instance, stirred to make an all-new album just three times in the 1980s and thrice more during the 1990s. [...] Genesis however, was not like "other bands"; it did not thrive in silence." It is once again Phil Collins, who separates his band from other bands they have been compared with, when he told *Sounds* in 1980: "I do feel that Tull are redundant, I can't think of anything Led Zeppelin have done in recent years that's progressed them. I find Floyd very boring – there's more substance in what we're doing" (Bowler & Dray 1992: 165). Bowler & Dray agree, thinking that "Genesis were the only band to go the distance with their artistic integrity intact." Phil Collins says that "we're constantly questioning ourselves much more than any of the lot" (Waller 1985: 86). In the documentary *Genesis "Granada Documentary" Part 2 (Duke's tour 1980)* he explains that "we've always been [...] unaffected by trends and fashions in music, really. And we've always made the music we want to make" (5:08). And in an interview from 1982 (*Phil Collins – Interview Clip – re Genesis music*) he sums up:

> "I still think that our music...you have to give it a time to get under your skin. [...] You can still listen to it maybe ten times [...], like a film, a good film or a book. [...] A good film, you should better see it three or four times

and still get something out of it. And I think that our music […] is a bit like that. We feel it is" (00:00).

And the last words come from Tony Banks, the heart and the soul of Genesis: "I think we are very different from track to track and album to album. […] I'm sometimes amazed at how little groups break out of their particular areas. I'd find that very restricting" (Fielder 1984: 122).

In September 2014, the band released another Best-Of: the 37-track set *R-Kive* (cf. http://www.genesis-music.com/), which features a chronological journey through the band history, including solo numbers from Banks, Collins, Gabriel, Hackett and Rutherford. One can see very nicely the development of the band's music and each member's influence.

In a radio interview, Mike Rutherford says that "from this one school band, Genesis, you had the Gabriel career, the Collins career, the **Mike + the Mechanics** career and you put these songs together and you see a…'Turn It On [Again]' and a 'Biko' and 'In the Air [Tonight]' 'Living Years,' it's a great body of work. I think we're trying to just remind people that we always were one band, really, one sort of team in a sense. And so, when you put it like that, I think it's a nice story to be told" (cf. http://www.classichitsandoldies.com/v2/2014/09/30/mike-rutherford-says-genesis-new-r-kive-compilation-showcases-a-great-body-of-work/). It is a signal to fans to rethink their narrow bounds and open up to the great music that came from the whole Genesis family over the years.

7. Afterglow: List of references

7.1 Looking For Someone: Primary sources

7.1.1 Videos

Abacab – Mama Tour – Genesis – 1984 – HQ:
https://www.youtube.com/watch?v=nE2EV1gqIk4, uploaded by Elio Reyes
on 1 October 2009. Web. 4 October 2014.

Ace Of Wands – Steve Hackett:
http://www.youtube.com/watch?v=EGu0JhYjRmo, uploaded by
python7275 on 28 March 2011. Web. 4 October 2014.

Genesis – Abacab 1981:
https://www.youtube.com/watch?v=5BSEbDEW8_k, uploaded by
memorylane1980s on 1 January 2011. Web. 4 October 2014.

Genesis – Dodo Suite: https://www.youtube.com/watch?v=l--bZDQMrSI,
uploaded by zizzu3782 on 8 December 2011. Web. 4 October 2014.

Genesis – Down and Out/From the Undertow:
http://www.youtube.com/watch?v=XKmk4LK3ov8, uploaded by zizzu3782
on 8 December 2011. Web. 4 October 2014.

Genesis – Duke's Suite: http://www.youtube.com/watch?v=Kd0jBZSeBjg,
uploaded by Matteo301297 on 6 January 2012. Web. 4 October 2014.

Genesis – Follow you, follow me:
https://www.youtube.com/watch?v=h9zj11gf9Qk, uploaded by too0pathetic
on 21 October 2010. Web. 4 October 2014.

Genesis – Full Concert Live in London (Duke Tour May 6 & 7, 1980):
http://www.youtube.com/watch?v=YbNo14hMuU8, uploaded by
JPDanley's channel on 29 December 2012. Web. 4 October 2014.

Genesis "Granada Documentary" Part 2 (Duke's tour 1980):
https://www.youtube.com/watch?v=UtSk-RbKuHY, uploaded by
TheRipples70 on 10 January 2012. Web. 20 January 2015.

Genesis…Home By The Sea "Live":
https://www.youtube.com/watch?v=8ibOkBudIHg, uploaded by Tony Mort
on 7 June 2013. Web. 4 October 2014.

Genesis – I can't dance (1991):
http://www.youtube.com/watch?v=qOyF4hR5GoE; uploaded by
too0pathetic on 17 July 2010. Web. 4 October 2014.

Genesis – I Know What I Like 1976 Live Video:
http://www.youtube.com/watch?v=eK9a2jLEAfs, uploaded by NEA
ZIXNH on 11 February 2014. Web. 4 October 2014.

Genesis – I Know What I Like (lyric):
http://www.youtube.com/watch?v=Za6DWVasjTw, uploaded by Wong Pak
Sam on 12 October 2013. Web. 4 October 2014.

Genesis – Invisible Touch (Invisible Touch Tour):
https://www.youtube.com/watch?v=cK3N2DC3Fds, uploaded by
PhilGenesisDB on 14 December 2008. Web. 4 October 2014.

Genesis – Invisible Touch [Official Music Video]:
https://www.youtube.com/watch?v=pW68T84RLHw, uploaded by
MrPhil46 on 9 April 2011. Web. 4 October 2014.

Genesis – Land Of Confusion [Official Music Video]:
http://www.youtube.com/watch?v=1pkVLqSaahk, uploaded by MrPhil46
on 29 March 2011. Web. 4 October 2014.

Genesis Live 1976 with Bill Bruford: Supper's Ready (Pt. II):
http://www.youtube.com/watch?v=0FrFytItybk, uploaded by
pistachoatomico on 17 September 2009. Web. 4 October 2014.

Genesis Live in London '80 Dance On A Volcano~Los Endos:
http://www.youtube.com/watch?v=hW66dxbgXS4, uploaded by
蛇銘多親父 on 24 July 2012. Web. 4 October 2014.

Genesis Mama Tour – Turn it on Again – Final Medley:
http://www.youtube.com/watch?v=BfaOqnWcIoc, uploaded by Agustin
dos Santos on 30 July 2012. Web. 4 October 2014.

Genesis – Misunderstanding (Three Sides Live) HQ:
http://www.youtube.com/watch?v=OLH32F6Xvkw, uploaded by
PhilGenesisDB on 26 November 2008. Web. 4 October 2014.

Genesis "Musical Box" (Seconds Out 1977):
http://www.youtube.com/watch?v=Ap-6KLzdfFI, uploaded by
TheRipples70 on 18 January 2012. Web. 4 October 2014.

Genesis-No Admittance-(1991)-Part 2:
https://www.youtube.com/watch?v=V8IVml6Wp_s, uploaded by
eurochrissy2 on 22 May 2012. Web. 20 January 2015.

Genesis-No Admittance-(1991)-Part 3:
https://www.youtube.com/watch?v=YCY2nT8x1ME, uploaded by
eurochrissy2 on 22 May 2012. Web. 20 January 2015.

Genesis-No Admittance (1991)-Part 4:
https://www.youtube.com/watch?v=LXxPbW70RSY, uploaded by
eurochrissy on 22 May 2012. Web. 28 January 2015.

Genesis – Supper's Ready (Live):
http://www.youtube.com/watch?v=M58wE8GTGp4, uploaded by Canale di
Francescodraghi1989 on 31 March 2011. Web. 4 October 2014.

Genesis - The Musical Box, Belgian TV – Six Hours Live:
http://www.youtube.com/watch?v=W35wtfcByIY, uploaded by
Tommygun1028 on 22 August 2007. Web. 4 October 2014.

Genesis – "Three Dates With Genesis" from BBC1 [1978]:
https://www.youtube.com/watch?v=HTLZ_yhVLXE, uploaded by
AlternativoPT451 on 11 June 2011. Web. 15 February 2015.

Genesis – Three Sides Live – Interview (part 1):
https://www.youtube.com/watch?v=CRP8c0-PLMc, uploaded by
LonelyManOnTheCorner on 22 April 2008. Web 22 January 2015.

Genesis – Throwing It All Away:
http://www.youtube.com/watch?v=xaENa3XdOAY, uploaded by emimusic
on 27 February 2009. Web. 4 October 2014.

Genesis – Turn It On Again (Live):
http://www.youtube.com/watch?v=kfCRv_4NuWk, uploaded by VidZone
on 13 March 2009. Web. 4 October 2014.

Genesis – When In Rome – Come Rain Or Shine HD:
https://www.youtube.com/watch?v=a9FuWw8ZuDo, uploaded by Jurand J
on 08 August 2013. Web. 16 January 2015.

Mike And The Mechanics – Silent Running (Music Video 1985):
http://www.youtube.com/watch?v=ttJsuLmcmiY, uploaded by Alisa Monee
Alvarez on 9 April 2011. Web. 4 October 2014.

MTV Genesis/Friday Night Video Fights 1983 Promo:
https://www.youtube.com/watch?v=2MZgnNry2Tc, uploaded by John
Quinn on 15 January 2012. Web. 15 February 2015.

Over My Shoulder (1995) – Mike + the Mechanics – Voc. Paul Carrack:
http://www.youtube.com/watch?v=tKiLGysBO7U, uploaded by
etnopollino on 9 June 2011. Web. 4 October 2014.

Peter Gabriel – Biko (1987): https://www.youtube.com/watch?v=MgM-
1r0X5Zc, uploaded by Genesis Channel on 12 August 2008. Web. 4 October
2014.

Peter Gabriel – Signal to Noise:
http://www.youtube.com/watch?v=xJoSNZxLdbU, uploaded by Pursche70
on 3 February 2010. Web. 8 October 2014.

Peter Gabriel – Solsbury Hill:
https://www.youtube.com/watch?v=_OO2PuGz-H8, uploaded by Peter
Gabriel on 20 May 2012. Web. 4 October 2014.

Peter Gabriel – Wogan 1987:
https://www.youtube.com/watch?v=Jl9At0qADuY, uploaded by 1967ngre
on 30 March 2012. Web. 16 January 2015.

Peter Gabriel on The South Bank Show 1983, Making of Security:
https://www.youtube.com/watch?v=scmYG1Pv1_Q, uploaded by
TheGenesisArchive on 14 July 2013. Web. 16 January 2015.

Phil Collins – In The Air Tonight (Official Video):
http://www.youtube.com/watch?v=YkADj0TPrJA, uploaded by Phil Collins
Official Channel on 11 May 2010. Web. 4 October 2014.

Phil Collins – Interview Clip – re Genesis music:
https://www.youtube.com/watch?v=tSgiHNXY5lA, uploaded by
MeanAuntie on 5 November 2006. Web. 22 January 2015.

Phil Collins – Wake Up Call (Official Music Video):
http://www.youtube.com/watch?v=XwzID90zhAc, uploaded by Phil
Collins Official Channel on 12 May 2010. Web. 4 October 2014.

Phil Collins & Philip Bailey "EASY LOVER" Subtitulado al español:
http://www.youtube.com/watch?v=UFrbMfBOiYY, uploaded by
collinstestify81 on 11 June 2013. Web. 4 October 2014.

Phil Collins & Genesis – Mama (Knebworth 1990):
http://www.youtube.com/watch?v=uqv_ccG6yOo, uploaded by MrPhil46
on 9 March 2011. Web. 4 October 2014.

phil collins – i missed again (home demo 1980):
https://www.youtube.com/watch?v=Fa5CL-UZXM0, uploaded by
derneueuntergang on 3 May 2009. Web. 6 January 2015.

Phil Collins Tonight Show 1985:
https://www.youtube.com/watch?v=rB9W2WfeuQE, uploaded by
carvcom1 on 9 March 2013. Web. 22 January 2015.

Phil Collins This Is Your Life: https://www.youtube.com/watch?v=-
Irpy0zHfis, uploaded by Mostly Floyd on 12 June 2014. Web. 22 January
2014.

Steve Hackett – Every Day:
http://www.youtube.com/watch?v=SQaGCNGgfe4, uploaded by
GordonYYZ on 17 November 2008. Web. 4 October 2014.

Steve Hackett – Nomads: http://www.youtube.com/watch?v=K5XH4Vt-
xHY, uploaded by ProgSympho on 7 June 2013. Web. 4 October 2014.

The Lamb Lies Down On Broadway – Genesis [Full Remastered Album] (1974): https://www.youtube.com/watch?v=MRSgvfNZcWA, uploaded by Hunter Koester on 4 December 2013. Web. 4 October 2014.

The Living Years (1988) – Mike + the Mechanics – Voc. Paul Carrack: http://www.youtube.com/watch?v=APXwdkdhC2c, uploaded by etnopollino on 12 June 2011. Web. 4 October 2014.

The Making of the Mama Album {DVD Bonus Disc} – Genesis [Movie Box] (1984): https://www.youtube.com/watch?v=iMm-08uZXfo, uploaded by Hunter Koester on 25 February 2014. Web. 16 January 2015.

Tony Banks – For A While (1979): http://www.youtube.com/watch?v=VRz7ZByNC58, uploaded by Genesis Channel on 19 November 2011. Web. 4 October 2014.

Tony Banks Interview May 1, 2012: https://www.youtube.com/watch?v=cmVrjYo01LI, uploaded by Banksian Central on 28 May 2012. Web. 22 January 2015.

Tony Banks & Phil Collins Interview December 24, 1976: https://www.youtube.com/watch?v=pCPrec5Rit0, uploaded by Banksian Central on 25 December 2014. Web. 22 January 2015.

Tony Banks – Siren (2012): http://www.youtube.com/watch?v=Xl23zqz79bQ, uploaded by 2poziomka on 15 April 2013. Web. 4 October 2014.

Tony Banks – Still – Red Day on Blue Street: http://www.youtube.com/watch?v=sy6PNg5Nt-U, uploaded by Banksian Central on 1 July 2011. Web. 4 October 2014.

Turn it on again medley – Live Knebworth – 1990 – Genesis: https://www.youtube.com/watch?v=TLVbogL3NLw, uploaded by Elio Reyes on 13 October 2008. Web. 4 October 2014.

7.1.2 Lyrics

Banks, Tony. For A While:
http://www.oldielyrics.com/lyrics/tony_banks/for_a_while.html, Web. 11
October 2014.

Banks, Tony. Red Day On Blue Street:
http://www.oldielyrics.com/lyrics/tony_banks/red_day_on_blue_street.htm
l, Web. 11 October 2014.

Collins, Phil. Easy Lover:
http://www.oldielyrics.com/lyrics/phil_collins/easy_lover.html, Web. 11
October 2014.

Collins, Phil. I Missed Again:
http://www.oldielyrics.com/lyrics/phil_collins/i_missed_again.html, Web.
11 October 2014.

Collins, Phil. In The Air Tonight:
http://www.oldielyrics.com/lyrics/phil_collins/in_the_air_tonight.html,
Web. 11 October 2014.

Collins, Phil. That's Just The Way It Is:
http://www.oldielyrics.com/lyrics/phil_collins/thats_just_the_way_it_is.ht
ml, Web. 11 October 2014.

Collins, Phil. Wake Up Call:
http://www.oldielyrics.com/lyrics/phil_collins/wake_up_call.html, Web. 11
October 2014.

Gabriel, Peter. Biko:
http://www.oldielyrics.com/lyrics/peter_gabriel/biko.html, Web. 11 October
2014.

Gabriel, Peter. Blood Of Eden:
http://www.oldielyrics.com/lyrics/peter_gabriel/blood_of_eden.html, Web.
11 October 2014.

Gabriel, Peter. Modern Love:
http://www.oldielyrics.com/lyrics/peter_gabriel/modern_love.html, Web.
11 October 2014.

Gabriel, Peter. Moribund The Burgermeister:
http://www.oldielyrics.com/lyrics/peter_gabriel/moribund_the_burgermeis
ter.html, Web. 11 October 2014.

Gabriel, Peter. Signal To Noise:
http://www.oldielyrics.com/lyrics/peter_gabriel/signal_to_noise.html, Web.
11 October 2014.

Gabriel, Peter. Solsbury Hill:
http://www.oldielyrics.com/lyrics/peter_gabriel/solsbury_hill.html, Web. 11
October 2014.

Genesis. Abacab: http://www.oldielyrics.com/lyrics/genesis/abacab.html,
Web. 11 October 2014.

Genesis. Afterglow:
http://www.oldielyrics.com/lyrics/genesis/afterglow.html, Web. 11 October
2014.

Genesis. Blood On The Rooftops:
http://www.oldielyrics.com/lyrics/genesis/blood_on_the_rooftops.html,
Web. 11 October 2014.

Genesis. Domino, Part I: In The Glow Of The Night:
http://www.oldielyrics.com/lyrics/genesis/domino_part_one_-
_in_the_glow_of_the_night.html, Web. 11 October 2014.

Genesis. Domino, Part II: The Last Domino:
http://www.oldielyrics.com/lyrics/genesis/domino_part_two_-
_the_last_domino.html, Web. 11 October 2014.

Genesis: Driving The Last Spike:
http://www.oldielyrics.com/lyrics/genesis/driving_the_last_spike.html,
Web. 11 October 2014.

Genesis. Dusk: http://www.oldielyrics.com/lyrics/genesis/dusk.html, Web.
11 October 2014.

Genesis: Follow You Follow Me.
http://www.oldielyrics.com/lyrics/genesis/follow_you_follow_me.html,
Web .11 October 2014.

Genesis. Home By The Sea:
http://www.oldielyrics.com/lyrics/genesis/home_by_the_sea.html, Web. 11
October 2014.

Genesis. I Can't Dance:
http://www.oldielyrics.com/lyrics/genesis/i_cant_dance.html, Web. 11
October 2014.

Genesis. I Know What I Like (In Your Wardrobe):
http://www.oldielyrics.com/lyrics/genesis/i_know_what_i_like_in_your_w
ardrobe.html, Web. 11 October 2014.

Genesis. Invisible Touch:
http://www.oldielyrics.com/lyrics/genesis/invisible_touch.html, Web. 11
October 2014.

Genesis. Jesus He Knows Me:
http://www.oldielyrics.com/lyrics/genesis/jesus_he_knows_me.html, Web.
11 October 2014.

Genesis. Land Of Confusion:
http://www.oldielyrics.com/lyrics/genesis/land_of_confusion.html, Web. 11
October 2014.

Genesis. Mama: http://www.oldielyrics.com/lyrics/genesis/mama.html,
Web. 11 October 2014.

Genesis. Misunderstanding:
http://www.oldielyrics.com/lyrics/genesis/misunderstanding.html, Web. 11
October 2014.

Genesis. One For The Vine:
http://www.oldielyrics.com/lyrics/genesis/one_for_the_vine.html, Web. 11
October 2014.

Genesis. Piper Club Rome 18 April 1972:
https://www.youtube.com/watch?v=XcnkjvHXwaU, Web. 8 December
2014.

Genesis. Ripples: http://www.oldielyrics.com/lyrics/genesis/ripples.html,
Web. 11 October 2014.

Genesis. Second Home By The Sea:
http://www.oldielyrics.com/lyrics/genesis/second_home_by_the_sea.html,
Web. 11 October 2014.

Genesis. Squonk: http://www.oldielyrics.com/lyrics/genesis/squonk.html,
Web. 11 October 2014.

Genesis. Stagnation:
http://www.oldielyrics.com/lyrics/genesis/stagnation.html, Web. 11
October 2014.

Genesis. Supper's Ready:
http://www.oldielyrics.com/lyrics/genesis/suppers_ready.html, Web 11
October 2014.

Genesis. The Knife:
http://www.oldielyrics.com/lyrics/genesis/the_knife.html, Web. 11 October
2014.

Genesis. The Lamb Lies Down On Broadway:
http://www.oldielyrics.com/lyrics/genesis/the_lamb_lies_down_on_broadw
ay.html, Web. 11 October 2014.

Genesis. The Musical Box:
http://www.oldielyrics.com/lyrics/genesis/the_musical_box.html, Web. 11
October 2014.

Genesis. Turn It On Again:
http://www.oldielyrics.com/lyrics/genesis/turn_it_on_again.html, Web. 11
October 2014.

Genesis. Visions Of Angels:
http://www.oldielyrics.com/lyrics/genesis/visions_of_angels.html, Web. 11
October 2014.

Genesis. White Mountain:
http://www.oldielyrics.com/lyrics/genesis/white_mountain.html, Web. 11
October 2014.

Hackett, Steve. Can't Let Go:
http://www.oldielyrics.com/lyrics/steve_hackett/cant_let_go.html, Web. 11
October 2014.

Hackett, Steve. Carry On Up The Vicarage: http://www.oldielyrics.com/lyrics/steve_hackett/carry_on_up_the_vicarage. html, Web. 11 October 2014.

Hackett, Steve. Everyday: http://www.oldielyrics.com/lyrics/steve_hackett/everyday.html, Web. 11 October 2014.

Hackett, Steve. Narnia: http://www.oldielyrics.com/lyrics/steve_hackett/narnia.html, Web. 11 October 2014.

Hackett, Steve. Nomads: http://www.oldielyrics.com/lyrics/steve_hackett/nomads.html, Web. 11 October 2014.

Mike and the Mechanics. Over My Shoulder: http://www.oldielyrics.com/lyrics/mike_and_the_mechanics/over_my_sho ulder.html, Web. 11 October 2014.

Mike and the Mechanics. Silent Running: http://www.oldielyrics.com/lyrics/mike_and_the_mechanics/silent_running .html, Web. 11 October 2014.

Mike and the Mechanics. The Living Years: http://www.oldielyrics.com/lyrics/mike_and_the_mechanics/the_living_yea rs.html, Web. 11 October 2014.

Phillips, Anthony. Birdsong: http://www.anthonyphillips.co.uk/lyrics/wise.htm#birdsong, Web. 11 October 2014.

Phillips, Anthony. God If I Saw Her Now: http://www.anthonyphillips.co.uk/lyrics/geese.htm#god, Web. 11 October 2014.

Phillips, Anthony. Magdalen: http://www.anthonyphillips.co.uk/lyrics/sides.htm#magdalen, Web. 11 October 2014.

Phillips, Anthony. We're All As We Lie:
http://www.anthonyphillips.co.uk/lyrics/wise.htm#waawl, Web. 11 October
2014.

7.1.3 Pictures

Banks, Tony. A Curious Feeling. Album cover:
http://www.progarchives.com/progressive_rock_discography_covers/833/c
over_54317182009.jpg, Web. 11 October 2014.

Banks, Tony. Soundtracks. Album cover:
http://www.progarchives.com/progressive_rock_discography_covers/833/c
over_343817182009.jpg, Web. 11 October 2014.

Collins, Phil. But Seriously. Album cover: http://www.philcollins-
fr.com/Discographie/albums/04butseriously.jpg, Web. 11 October 2014.

Collins, Phil. Hits. Album cover: http://www.philcollins-
fr.com/Discographie/albums/08hits.jpg, Web. 5 October 2014.

Gabriel, Peter. No Self Control. Single cover:
http://www.progarchives.com/progressive_rock_discography_covers/686/c
over_2329201692009.jpg Web. 5 October 2014.

Gabriel, Peter. Peter Gabriel Plays Live. Album cover:
http://www.progarchives.com/progressive_rock_discography_covers/686/c
over_4055163172009.jpg, Web. 5 October 2014.

Genesis. A trick of the tail. Album cover:
http://www.bluesnaggletooth12.com/lists-imgs/trick.jpg, Web. 11 October
2014.

Genesis. And Then There Were Three. Album cover:
http://1000plastinok.net/bigcovers/14445.jpeg, Web. 11 October 2014.

Genesis. Foxtrot. Album cover: http://basscatmusic.com/wp-
content/uploads/2013/09/Genesis-Foxtrot-Cover-BCM-800x400.png, Web.
11 October 2014.

Genesis. From Genesis to revelation. Album cover: http://images.gibson.com/Lifestyle/English/aaFeaturesImages2011/genesis_first1.jpg, Web. 11 October 2014.

Genesis. Invisible Touch. Album cover: http://www.progarchives.com/progressive_rock_discography_covers/1/cover_1145181162011_r.jpg, Web. 11 October 2014.

Genesis. Live. Album cover: http://www.genesismuseum.com/posters/liveposter.jpg, Web. 11 October 2014.

Genesis. Many too many. Single cover: http://farm6.static.flickr.com/5012/5577634078_9ee41ac2a0.jpg, Web. 11 October 2014.

Genesis. Nursery Cryme. Album cover: http://www.genesismuseum.com/vinyl/nc/lpcover.jpg, Web. 11 October 2014.

Genesis. Platinum Collection. Album cover: http://www.progarchives.com/progressive_rock_discography_covers/1/cover_12382318102008.jpg, Web. 11 October 2014.

Genesis. Selling England by the pound. Album cover: http://www.progarchives.com/progressive_rock_discography_covers/1/cover_404762112008.JPG, Web. 11 October 2014.

Genesis. The Lamb Lies Down On Broadway. Album cover: http://beatlesnumber9.com/lamb1.jpg, Web. 11 October 2014.

Genesis. Trespass. Album cover: http://www.soundstation.dk/images/products/large/80/133280-b.jpg, Web. 11 October 2014.

Genesis. Turn it on again. Single cover: http://www.progarchives.com/progressive_rock_discography_covers/1/cover_1317151712010.jpg, Web. 11 October 2014.

Genesis. Wind and Wuthering. Album cover:
http://www.getvinyl.com/img/original/7951.JPG, Web. 11 October 2014.

Hackett, Steve. Please Don't Touch. Album cover:
http://eil.com/images/main/Steve%2BHackett%2B-
%2BPlease%2BDon%27t%2BTouch%2B-
%2BBlue%2Blabel%2B%252B%2BLyric%2BInner%2B-%2BLP%2BRECORD-
554043.jpg, Web. 5 October 2014.

Hackett, Steve. Till We Have Faces. Album cover:
http://www.insideoutshop.de/images/products/large/0IO01096_6349472548
18037094.jpg, Web. 5 October 2014.

Mike and the Mechanics. M6. Album cover:
http://cdalameda.com/catalog/images/mike-the-mechanics-m6-1999-front-
cover-62170.jpg, Web. 5 October 2014.

Phillips, Anthony. The Geese and the ghost. Album cover:
http://www.progarchives.com/progressive_rock_discography_covers/779/c
over_470113172009.jpg, Web. 5 October 2014.

Phillips, Anthony. Wise After the event. Album cover:
http://www.anthonyphillips.co.uk/discography/wise300.jpg, Web. 5
October 2014.

Phillips, Anthony. Sides. Album cover:
http://www.progarchives.com/progressive_rock_discography_covers/779/c
over_2048103172009.jpg, Web. 5 October 2014.

Rutherford, Mike. Acting Very Strange. Single cover:
http://eil.com/images/main/Mike%2BRutherford%2B-
%2BActing%2BVery%2BStrange%2B-%2B7%2522%2BRECORD-577867.jpg,
Web. 11 October 2014.

7.2 Hand In Hand: Secondary Sources

Ameri, Many; Schmidt, Torsten: For the record. Conversations with people who have shaped the way we listen to music.

Banks, Tony; Collins, Phil; Gabriel, Peter; Hackett, Steve; Rutherford, Mike; Dodd, Philip (2007): Genesis. Chapter & verse. New York: Thomas Dunne Books/St. Martin's Griffin.

Bright, Spencer (1988): Peter Gabriel. An authorized biography. London: Sidgwick & Jackson.

Bowler, Dave; Dray, Bryan (1992): Genesis. A biography. London: Sidgwick & Jackson.

Brown, Adam Tod. "4 Famous Bands We (Wrongly) Hated When They Tried to Change." http://www.cracked.com/blog/4-famous-bands-we-wrongly-hated-when-they-tried-to-change/ 13 March 2014. cracked.com. 5 October 2014.

Currie, The Christopher. 1998. "Tentative reviews by The Christopher Currie: Genesis – The Lamb Lies Down On Broadway." http://www.tranglos.com/marek/yes/tr_77.html. 5 October 2014.

Currie, The Christopher. 1998. "Tentative reviews by The Christopher Currie: Genesis – We Can't Dance." http://www.tranglos.com/marek/yes/tr_91.html. 5 October 2014.

Eddins, Stephen. n.d. "Tony Banks – Six Pieces for Orchestra – City of Prague Philharmonic Orchestra, Paul Englishby." http://www.allmusic.com/album/tony-banks-six-pieces-for-orchestra-mw0002328064, Web. 5 October 2014.

Fielder, Hugh; Sutcliffe, Phil (1984): The book of Genesis. London: Sidgewick & Jackson.

Gabrielli, Giulia in Keazor, Henry; Wübbena, Thorsten (2010): Rewind, play, fast forward. The past, present and future of the music video. Bielfield, Piscataway, NJ: Transaction Publishers (Cultural and media studies).

Gallo, Armando (1978): Genesis. Köln: Böhler.

"Genesis – Behind The Music Remastred":
https://www.youtube.com/watch?v=CJhigbxwEIw, uploaded by
RockerRollin84 on 30 August 2013. Web. 4 October 2014.

"Genesis interviewed on The Lamb Lies Down on Broadway":
http://www.youtube.com/watch?v=srJqb2RHFq0, uploaded by progrock70s
on 24 August 2013. Web. 5 October 2014.

"Genesis News Com [it]: Steve Hackett – Out Of The Tunnels Mouth – CD
Review: http://www.genesis-news.com/c-Steve-Hackett-Out-Of-The-
Tunnels-Mouth-CD-review-s348.html, n.p., n.d. Web. 5 October 2014.

"GENESIS: SONGBOOK part 1":
http://www.youtube.com/watch?v=e1nQp-IlJ7Q, uploaded by "ABOUT
MUSIC - Roma, Via Frattina 52 - Official Music Merchandise Shop" on 28
November 2013. Web. 4 October 2014.

"Genesis – The Invisible Touch Tour":
https://www.youtube.com/watch?v=rporQN-QTgk, uploaded by
AlternativoPT451 on 8 June 2011. Web. 4 October 2014.

Gordon, Stewart (1996): A history of keyboard literature. Music for the
piano and its forerunners. New York, London: Schirmer Books; Prentice
Hall International.

Grout, Donald Jay; Burkholder, J. Peter; Palisca, Claude V. (2005): A history
of western music. Princeton, N.J: Recording for the Blind & Dyslexic.

Halbscheffel, Bernward (2013): Progressive Rock. Die ernste Musik der
Popmusik. Leipzig: Halbscheffel

Haynes, Bruce (2007): The end of early music. A period performer's history
of music for the twenty-first century. Oxford, New York: Oxford University
Press.

Hegarty, Paul; Halliwell, Martin (2011): Beyond and before. Progressive
rock since the 1960s. New York: Continuum.

Holm-Hudson, Kevin (2008): Genesis and the lamb lies down on Broadway. Aldershot, England, Burlington, VT: Ashgate

Holmes, Thom (1985): Electronic and experimental music. New York: Scribner's (The Scribner music library)

Jackson, Terry. 2012. Tony Banks – "Still" Review. http://www.prognaut.com/reviews/tony-banks2.html, Web. 5 October 2014.

Keazor, Henry; Wübbena, Thorsten (2010): Rewind, play, fast forward. The past, present and future of the music video. Bielfield, Piscataway, NJ: Transaction Publishers (Cultural and media studies).

Mackerness, E. D. (1966): A Social History of English Music. 2. Ed. London: Routledge and Kegan Paul.

Masters, Tim. 2014. Peter Gabriel honoured at Prog music awards. http://www.bbc.com/news/entertainment-arts-29159619, Web. 6 December 2014.

McMahan, Scott. 1998. The Genesis Discography 1967-1996: "The scattered pages of a book by the sea ..." http://cyberreviews.skwc.com/gendis.pdf Web. 5 October 2014.

"Mike Rutherford Says Genesis' New "R-Kive" Compilation Showcases "a Great Body of Work" http://www.classichitsandoldies.com/v2/2014/09/30/mike-rutherford-says-genesis-new-r-kive-compilation-showcases-a-great-body-of-work/

"Music: Land of Confusion – Television Tropes and Idioms." http://tvtropes.org/pmwiki/pmwiki.php/Music/LandOfConfusion, n.p., n.d. Web. 4 October 2014.

Peverini, Paolo in Keazor, Henry; Wübbena, Thorsten (2010): Rewind, play, fast forward. The past, present and future of the music video. Bielfield, Piscataway, NJ: Transaction Publishers (Cultural and media studies).

Phillips, Anthony. A Catch At The Tables. http://www.anthonyphillips.co.uk/discography/pp4.htm 3 February 2014. Web. 5 October 2014.

Phillips, Anthony. Twelve.
http://www.anthonyphillips.co.uk/discography/pp5.htm, 3 February 2014.
Web. 5 October 2014.

Platts, Robin (2007): Genesis. Behind the lines, 1967-2007. Burlington, Ont.,
Canada: Collectors Guide Pub.

Room, Adrian (1990): An A to Z of British life. Oxford: Oxford University
Press.

Russell, Paul (2004): Genesis. A live guide, 1969-1975. London, England:
SAF.

Stardust. "Supper's Ready vs The Duke Suite." Forum thread:
http://genesisgts.conforums.com/index.cgi?board=music&action=display&n
um=1390044159, 18 January 2014. Web. 4 October 2014.

Thompson, Andy (1999 – 2004): "Planet Mellotron Album Reviews:
Genesis." http://www.planetmellotron.com/revgenesis.htm, n.d. Web. 4
October 2014.

Thompson, Dave (2005): Turn it on again. Peter Gabriel, Phil Collins &
Genesis. San Francisco: Backbeat Books.

"Tony Banks Interview from 'Genesis: A History'":
https://www.youtube.com/watch?v=Wuze8WBZ648, uploaded by Banksian
Central on 16 November 2013. Web. 4 October 2014.

"Tony Banks Interview from 'Genesis Songbook DVD'":
https://www.youtube.com/watch?v=zFwJhQt7RRg, uploaded by Banksian
Central on 5 May 2014, Web. 4 October 2014.

Waller, Johnny (1985): The Phil Collins story. London, Port Chester, N.Y.:
Zomba Books.

Welch, Chris (2005): Genesis. The complete guide to their music. London:
Omnibus Press.